MULVANE
ON THE PROD

Center Point
Large Print

Also by William Heuman and available from Center Point Large Print:

Guns at Broken Bow
On to Santa Fe
Then Came Mulvane
Gunhand from Texas
Bullets for Mulvane
Roll the Wagons
Hunt the Man Down
Hardcase Halloran
The Range Buster
Ride for Texas

MULVANE ON THE PROD

WILLIAM HEUMAN

CENTER POINT LARGE PRINT
THORNDIKE, MAINE

This Center Point Large Print edition
is published in the year 2025 by arrangement with
Golden West Inc.

Copyright © 1962 by William Heuman.

All rights reserved.

The text of this Large Print edition is unabridged.
In other aspects, this book may vary
from the original edition.
Printed in the United States of America
on permanent paper sourced using
environmentally responsible foresting methods.
Set in 16-point Times New Roman type.

ISBN: 979-8-89164-518-9

The Library of Congress has cataloged this record
under Library of Congress Control Number: 2024951740

CHAPTER 1

Mulvane had supposed that Charlie O'Leary might have company when he'd decided to drop in on the little rancher, but he had not anticipated that the company would consist of about thirty or more armed men surrounding the shack along Elbow Creek and pouring lead into it from every side. O'Leary, part time rancher, part time rustler, and full time good comrade, was a congenial little man who picked up friends the way a shaggy dog picked up burrs, but Mulvane was quite sure that Charlie had not invited this crowd firing down on him from the wooded slopes on both sides of the creek.

Carefully, Mulvane pulled the claybank back in among the trees and he stared down at the shack a hundred and fifty yards away. Coming through El Dorado Pass that afternoon he'd heard the cannonade from a considerable distance but had not supposed that it was centering around Charlie O'Leary's humble abode.

There was no doubt that Charlie still lived here along Elbow Creek a few miles from the cattle town of Wickburg because every once in a while the little rancher let out a disdainful whoop as he fired his rifle first through one shattered window and then another, keeping this small army at bay. Charlie could be quite cheerful even in this dire predicament because he still had an ace card up his sleeve. On his previous visit to this place several years ago Mulvane had been taken through a little tunnel which led from underneath the floor of Charlie's shack out to the creek bank some seventy-five yards away.

"Dug by the last rancher had this place," Charlie had explained as he'd pushed his way through the brush opening on the creek bank. "Had plenty o' Injuns around in them days, an' he figured it would come in handy."

The tunnel would certainly be coming in handy this day, Mulvane knew, because the riflemen surrounding the shack were moving in closer all the time. Several of them were already up close to the pole corral less than a hundred feet from the house. The others were crawling down along the slopes, finding protection behind the trees, and it would only be a matter of minutes before Charlie had to take to his tunnel.

Mulvane surmised that the little man had hoped to hold out until dusk when he could more easily elude the gunmen surrounding his place. Now it would definitely be a risk when he emerged from the tunnel exit.

As Mulvane watched from the fringe of trees, a rider moved past him at a distance of fifty feet. The rider sat very stiff and straight in the saddle, a military carriage distinctly unlike the easy, slouching posture of the ordinary cowhand in this part of Wyoming Territory. The rider was a big fellow with grizzled, graying hair and a craggy face. Both horse and rider quite surprised Mulvane. The horse was a huge black stallion with a dead white face, the oddest combination Mulvane had ever seen.

The brand on the animal's flank, also, was very distinctive and undoubtedly new to this country. It consisted of intercrossed right angles inside a circle.

Waiting until the rider had disappeared among the trees, Mulvane started to circle leisurely in the direction of the tunnel exit, knowing that Charlie would need help when he emerged. He would also need a horse because he certainly would not be bringing a horse through the tunnel.

Most of the crew surrounding the shack were on foot which meant that they had tied their mounts somewhere in the vicinity. Riding through the trees Mulvane kept a sharp eye out for the horses, and then quite unexpectedly as he entered a clearing, a rider emerged from the trees on the other side and came straight toward him.

There was no time to avoid the man, and knowing that he had already been seen, Mulvane calmly rode directly toward him. The second rider was astride a sorrel horse and was evidently just coming to this affair, riding up in haste, and yanking a Winchester from a saddle holster as he did so.

As he drew near, Mulvane lifted a hand for him to stop. He said easily, "Plenty of them on the other side. Reckon you'd better move down the grade here and close in on him."

The rider, a tall, raw-boned fellow with a growth of dark fuzz on his face, stared at Mulvane uncertainly for one moment and then nodded as he stepped from the saddle. Reaching for the bridle Mulvane said, "I'll take your horse back with the others. Get in as close as you can, and look sharp. The little devil can shoot like hell."

The tall fellow mumbled something about, "shootin' the hell out o' him," and then he started down the grade in the direction of the shack, skipping in and out among the trees.

Whistling tunelessly, Mulvane rode on leading the sorrel. He tied both horses in a thicket some distance back from the creek at a point near where the tunnel opened. Then he moved forward on foot, working his way down toward the creek and trying to remember exactly where the opening had been.

The crew surrounding the shack were still firing at it, but Mulvane could no longer hear Charlie's return fire which meant that either he'd been hit or he'd already gone down through the trap door and was now heading out toward the creek.

Elder Creek was fifteen feet across, studded

with stones, and had five-foot banks on either side covered with willows. Stepping across the creek on stones, Mulvane headed north, keeping his head down below the rim of the creek bank just in case Charlie spotted him from the shack and sent a bullet in his direction.

He passed one man who was flattened against the bank, a rifle pushed through the brush. When the rifleman turned to look at him, Mulvane said in a low voice, "Keep your head down. I figure we winged him but he's still dangerous."

He kept going, not even looking back at the man on the bank, as he searched for the huge boulder in the creek bed which was his landmark. The boulder had been very close to the exit of the tunnel.

He came upon the boulder shortly, a man-high rock, quite round, and reddish in color, which split the creek. The banks were considerably higher here, well over six feet with the brush very thick. Unfortunately, one of the besiegers had taken up a position not more than ten feet from the tunnel exit.

Hearing Mulvane coming up along the gravelly bank of the creek, the rifleman turned around to stare at him. He was a short, stocky man with a very red face and light brown hair. He had a blond mustache beneath a bulbous nose, and his eyes were light blue.

Mulvane casually climbed up beside the man,

pushed aside the bushes, and stared in the direction of the shack, now very near. He said carelessly, "Keep your head down. He's still plenty dangerous."

"*Vas?*" the red-faced man asked, blue eyes blinking.

Mulvane looked at him curiously. "Reckon Charlie's hit," he said.

The stocky man shook his head uncomprehendingly, and then spoke very rapidly in a foreign tongue which Mulvane took to be German. The short man kept pointing toward the shack and then toward a rock close by his head where Mulvane could see a bullet had chipped off the edge. Evidently Charlie O'Leary had taken a bead on the red-faced foreigner not too long ago.

Mulvane held up both hands indicating that he did not understand what the German was saying. At the same time he found himself wondering at this strange situation. The big fellow on the black stallion had not ridden like a westerner, and this short man on the bank spoke no English. The tenor of this country had evidently changed in the three years since Mulvane had seen Charlie O'Leary. A foreign element seemed to have come in, and not only had it come in, but it had the whiphand.

Rolling over on his side Mulvane drew the makings from his shirt pocket and started to roll a cigarette as he eyed the brush which concealed the tunnel exit a short distance away. The stocky little German watched him as he got the cigarette going, and then Mulvane handed him the sack and the cigarette papers.

The German had evidently learned how to roll his own cigarettes and he accepted the packet gratefully. As he started to make his smoke Mulvane crawled up above him on the bank to have a look. He noticed that one of the men who had been up behind the corral had now crawled up and flattened himself behind an outhouse some half-dozen yards from the house. It was now only a matter of moments before they rushed the place. When they discovered that Charlie was gone they would immediately begin to search for him, which would make it much more difficult for Charlie when he came out of the tunnel.

Drawing his Colt from the holster, Mulvane waited until the German had the cigarette in his mouth and was putting a match to it, and then he smashed the gun barrel across the man's hat. The cigarette broke apart as the German's teeth clamped shut on it. He slid down the bank soundlessly, jaw sagging, the tobacco spilling over his shirt front.

Holstering the gun, Mulvane grasped the German by the arms and dragged him in among the willows where he would be concealed in case anyone passed by. He pushed his way toward the tunnel exit; then, pulling aside the bushes, he called softly, "Charlie—Charlie O'Leary?"

Little Charlie's head popped out almost immediately, a small, round face dirtied from the long crawl through the tunnel, and with blood on his left cheek where a bullet had grazed him. Charlie O'Leary was a short, roly-poly man with reddish hair, baby blue eyes, and a small stub nose. He said in a low voice, "Mulvane! Hells bells!"

"Kind of got you in a bind here," Mulvane smiled. "I have another horse back up the grade and we don't have too much time."

"Time for one thing," Charlie grinned. "Reckon I kin drink this creek dry."

Mulvane watched him as he slid down the bank to the creek and bent to drink heavily. He got up, wiping his mouth with the back of his sleeve, and nodded to Mulvane. Both men stepped across the creek and started up through the trees.

When they were some distance back from the creek Charlie said, "Reckon you come in the nick o' time, Mulvane. What brings you on this side o' the mountains?"

Mulvane shrugged. "Passing through," he said. "Figured I'd stop and see you, Charlie. That a posse after you or just plain, honest citizens fed up with your killing their beef for meat?"

"Hell," Charlie chuckled. "Ain't no harm in a man takin' a beeve now an' then. Some people got just too damned many, Mulvane."

They picked up the horses and rode down

creek, moving due east in the direction of Wickburg. Mulvane said when they were some distance away from the shack, "Figure you stole more than just a beeve, Charlie, to get that crowd on your back."

"The Dutchman's usin' me fer an example," Charlie explained. "Supposin' we grant fer the sake o' argument that I been takin' a beeve now an' then, no more than usual. Understand, Mulvane?"

"I understand," Mulvane nodded soberly.

"Now the Dutchman comes along an' he figures he owns the whole world," Charlie went on. "He sits in that damned stonepile on his hill lookin' down on the poor people like he was some god. He figures there's too many two-bit ranchers in this territory an' they're gittin' in his way. Way I look at it he figures on takin' over the whole state o' Wyoming afore he's through an' runnin' ten million cattle on it."

"Who is the Dutchman?" Mulvane asked.

"Herr Kurt Von Dreber," Charlie told him. "Tell me he's an ex–Prussian officer. Come out this way about two years ago with his own crowd from the Fatherland. Brung along stone masons to build his big stone castle way up on top of a hill, not like the rest of us down in the protected valley. He has a crowd o' smaller Dutchmen with him an' you ought to see 'em snap to attention an' lick his boots when he says so."

"The Dutchman," Mulvane mused. "Big man rides stiff and straight in the saddle? Rides a big black with a white face?"

Charlie nodded. "Damndest lookin' horse west o' the Missouri," he said. "Around here we call that animal the Death Horse. Some people say Von Dreber rode that animal right over poor Stan Jenkins who had a little spread up on Whistle Springs. Stan wouldn't run no more than I run when we got our orders to move out."

Mulvane stared down at the claybank's neck as they rode along. He said, "Von Dreber tells a man to leave and he's supposed to leave. Is that it, Charlie? Where's the law in this country?"

"Neil McAdams is the law in Wickburg," Charlie explained, "but Von Dreber bought him out or scared him out, one or the other. McAdams looks the other way when things get tough fer the small ranchers. Von Dreber kin allus say he's clearin' the country o' cattle rustlers like me an' Sam Holloway. Only we ain't rustlers, Mulvane. We take a beeve now an' then to keep our hands in the business but it don't mean anything. Von Dreber just wants to run us out so's he kin push that damned swastika brand all over the territory. You seen the brand on that big black?"

"Saw it," Mulvane nodded. He looked back, then, and he saw the column of smoke lifting toward the sky, and he said, "You're burned out,

Charlie. Where do you small ranchers go when Von Dreber chases you?"

"Into Wickburg," Charlie told him. "Only one not afraid to help us is Rosslyn Elder. She'll give me a stake if I ask fer one. Nobody else will on account o' the Dutchman's put the fear into 'em."

Mulvane scratched his chin. "She's another new one here since I last came through," he said.

"Runs the El Dorado Saloon and Gambling Hall," Charlie explained. "A square shooter. Got no use fer Von Dreber. She's been helpin' the boys who've been chased out."

They rode on for a while in silence and then Mulvane said, "You figure on pulling out, Charlie?"

"Hell no," Charlie laughed. "I owe that Dutchman one an' he's gonna get it."

"You damned near got it yourself this afternoon," Mulvane reminded him. "That bother you, Charlie?"

"Nobody lives forever," Charlie laughed. "Reckon you found that out, Mulvane."

"I found it out," Mulvane nodded soberly.

CHAPTER 2

It was mid-afternoon when Charlie O'Leary came out of the tunnel and it was nearly dusk when they rode into the town of Wickburg, Mulvane finding it considerably larger than it had been when he'd been here previously. In addition to a long, straggling main street there were two smaller cross streets, and at least half a dozen new saloons, a hotel, a bank, and now the big El Dorado Gambling Hall on the main corner, owned and operated by a Miss Rosslyn Elder.

"I figure she'll put me up at the El Dorado," Charlie said when Mulvane offered to get him a room at the hotel. "When the Dutchman's crowd finds I'm still alive they're liable to send Varney Baudine and some of his toughs to work me over. They won't dare do that at Miss Elder's because she has some toughs of her own on the payroll."

"Baudine ramrod for Von Dreber?" Mulvane asked.

"A tough one," Charlie nodded. "Bad man with a gun afore he came here, an' bigger since he's been in town. He does the dirty work for Von Dreber. Reckon you'll be seein' him soon enough 'cause there's been a few boys in that crowd around my place seen you. That Dutchman by the tunnel exit, for one."

Mulvane parted with Charlie out in front of the El Dorado and then he rode the claybank on to the Wickburg Hotel, stabled the horse in the rear, and engaged a room for himself on the second floor, the window overlooking the main street.

He washed and shaved and changed to a clean shirt, and then he went downstairs. Crossing the lobby he saw the most beautiful woman he'd ever seen in his life just coming in through the door. He stopped in his stride in spite of himself and stared at her before going on toward the dining room off the lobby.

The woman was quite tall, regal in every respect, dressed in a lavender and white traveling costume with a pert straw hat topped with a feather. She carried her head high, which made her look taller than she was. Her hair was silvery-blonde in color, with blue eyes to match. The nose and mouth were perfectly proportioned, and her teeth sparkled as she spoke. She looked almost unreal as she walked across the lobby toward the desk, accompanied by a retinue of servants, two female and two male, the four of them loaded down with portmanteaus and trunks which they had just taken from the westbound stage now standing outside the hotel.

The servants were all chattering away in German and trying to make themselves understood to the dazed clerk at the desk. As Mulvane paused at the dining room door he heard the tall blonde woman speaking to the clerk in perfect English, but with a very slight foreign accent. She was asking if she could have a meal served at the hotel while she was waiting to be picked up by Colonel Von Dreber. He heard her give her name as Countess Hilda Hannau.

A bewhiskered man standing near the dining room door, smelling strongly of liquor, said tersely as Mulvane went by, "Damned country's fillin' up with them Prussians. Reckon this is the queen the king's been waitin' for out on that hill."

In the dining room Mulvane found an empty table and ordered his supper from the waitress. He had not been at the table more than a minute when Countess Hilda Hannau stepped into the room, escorted by the clerk. She was given a table a short distance away, the clerk hurriedly summoning the waitress to take her order.

The woman's blue eyes passed over Mulvane briefly as she sat down. The drunk who'd made the remark to Mulvane at the door now moved up toward her table. He was a big, raw-boned man with a long jaw and the hands of a farmer.

Looking at him, Mulvane was quite sure that this was one of the ranchers or homesteaders Von Dreber had ruthlessly pushed from his land and hence turned into an habitual drunk.

The farmer paused at the Countess Hannau's table, and then quite suddenly he sat down in the chair across from her, the waitress staring at him, a little frightened. The big fellow pounded on the table with his fist and he said grimly, "You're all alike, walkin' around like you owned the earth, tellin' people what to do, drivin' 'em like they were cattle."

The Countess Hannau stared at the man coldly. She was not flustered, not afraid, and respect came into Mulvane's eyes as he watched her. She was a blueblood, and she would remain a blueblood.

He heard her say quietly, "Will you please leave. I do not wish to talk with you."

"You don't wish to talk with me!" the farmer roared. "Then I'll talk with you, lady, an' I'll tell you what I think of you damned foreigners who come over here an' try to run the country."

Mulvane had turned in his chair and was looking across at them. When the Countess Hannau glanced in his direction he got up, crossing to the table. He said, "Reckon that's it, mister. You better leave now."

The farmer stood up, eyes narrowed, rubbing his big hands on his pants. "You in this, Jack?" he asked.

"I'm in it," Mulvane smiled. "You're drunk, mister. Why not take a walk and then think it over."

"Get back to your table, Jack," the farmer rasped. "I'm talkin' to the lady."

"Not anymore," Mulvane told him, still smiling.

He was ready when the farmer made his move, and he was resolved to make it short and sweet for the big fellow's own sake. When the farmer swung a ponderous right hand, Mulvane pulled back his head, stepping lightly. He came up with his own right fist, catching the farmer full on the jaw and sending him crashing against the wall where he slid down, glassy-eyed.

Walking over and grasping him under the armpits Mulvane dragged him calmly to the street door, hauled him outside, and sat him against the wall.

When he came back into the dining room Countess Hannau nodded and smiled at him, flashing her white teeth. She said, "Join me."

It was more a command than an invitation. Mulvane sat down on the chair vacated by the farmer and he said, "You'll run across one or two like that in this part of the country, ma'am. They'll talk when they're drunk."

Countess Hannau nodded. "You are very efficient," she observed studying him appreciatively. "What is your name?"

"Mulvane," he told her, and even though he knew her name he said, "What is yours?"

Countess Hilda Hannau lifted her eyebrows momentarily as if surprised by the question because common people did not ordinarily ask her her name.

"I am the Countess Hilda Hannau of Saxony,"

she stated. "I have come to join my fiancé in this country."

"Mr. Von Dreber?" Mulvane asked.

"Colonel Von Dreber," the countess said. "Do you work for him? I understand he hires many men."

Mulvane shook his head. "Just rode in," he stated, and he wondered what Von Dreber would say when he learned that his fiancé was dining with a drifter.

The thought apparently did not disturb the Countess Hannau. She gave her order to the waitress and then requested that the girl serve Mulvane at her table. She said nothing then for several moments as she sat across from Mulvane, looking at him steadily and making him more and more uncomfortable as she did so.

There was a faint smile on her face as she said finally, "I do not suppose that in this country you are familiar with the writings of Friedrich Wilhelm Nietzsche?"

Mulvane shook his head, a little puzzled.

"Dr. Nietzsche is a German philosopher," the countess explained. "Both my fiancé and myself have accepted his teachings." She paused and then went on carefully, "I see in you, Herr Mulvane, the typical product of the new civilization we hope to introduce to the world."

Mulvane took a cigar out of his pocket and placed it on the table in front of him. He watched her, some humor in his gray eyes.

"You are strong, virile, and efficient," the Countess told him. "The ultimate object of Dr. Nietzsche's philosophy is to produce a race of men, or supermen, who shall rule the world and make it a better place in which to live."

Mulvane thought of Charlie O'Leary who had been burned out this afternoon, and who had luckily escaped with his life.

"What happens to those who are not supermen," he asked softly, "and who do not wish to become so?"

Countess Hannau waved a hand carelessly. "In time they shall disappear from the face of the earth," she said. "Our kind, yours and mine, shall rule. The meek shall not inherit the earth, only the strong and the powerful." She paused and added, "If you are not employed, Herr Mulvane, I would suggest that you go out to Valhalla with us. That is where the great experiment is to begin."

Mulvane said quietly, "If you wanted to develop a super race why didn't you attempt this in Prussia?"

Countess Hannau shrugged. "The Colonel feels that Europe is decadent with old philosophies and religions. In this new land, in the wide open West which is young, we can begin from the bottom."

Mulvane nodded. "In this country," he said, "when you step on the low man you step on all of us and we all fight back together. This is not

Europe. This is America where one man is as good as another, and we're ready to prove it." He stood up, then, his eyes cold, and he put the cigar back in his shirt pocket. He said, "This afternoon your fiancé and his friends tried to murder one little man. There were thirty or more against one. Is that the way you figure on producing your race of supermen?"

Countess Hannau was staring up at him, her beautiful lips slightly parted, too stunned for a moment to speak, and it was the first time he'd seen her lose her composure even momentarily.

Mulvane picked up his hat and walked back to his own table and sat down. He ate his dinner without again looking in her direction, conscious of the fact that a number of times she was staring at him.

He finished his dinner and paid his bill. As he was passing her table on the way out she put out a hand and touched his arm. When he looked down she was smiling at him warmly. She was all woman now and breathtakingly beautiful.

"If I have offended you, Herr Mulvane," she smiled, "I am indeed sorry. You must come out to Valhalla someday to visit us. You have done me a service this evening."

Mulvane nodded. "Obliged for the invitation," he said, and he went out into the street.

The town of Wickburg was filling up even though the hour was still young. There were horses tied in front of every tie rack along the street, and the big El Dorado Saloon and Gambling Hall seemed to be in full blast.

Charlie O'Leary had asked him to come down for a drink and Mulvane headed that way now. As he walked up the street he saw a buckboard, two powerful grays in harness, swinging down the main street in the direction of the hotel. The buckboard narrowly missed a small boy crossing the road.

Mulvane paused to stare at the buckboard as it rolled past. The driver had made no attempt whatever to slow down the big grays in the harness. He'd undoubtedly seen the boy, but the buckboard had kept rolling as if the boy had not been there.

As the rig rolled by through a patch of light from a nearby saloon Mulvane had a good look at the man with the reins, recognizing him immediately as the big fellow with the graying hair who had ridden the Death Horse out at Charlie's place that afternoon, and whom he'd later identified as Kurt Von Dreber.

Von Dreber had a face cut out of stone, a hard, rock-ribbed, square-jawed face with many curious small scars on the cheeks and chin, which Mulvane learned later had come from numerous student duels in Prussia.

The buckboard rolled up to the hotel and Von Dreber stepped down, walking into the lobby to meet his fiancée. The short, stocky man with Von Dreber Mulvane recognized as the Prussian he'd pistol-whipped outside the tunnel exit on the creek.

In the El Dorado, Charlie O'Leary was waiting for Mulvane at the bar.

"Drink's on me," Charlie grinned. "Hear you been gettin' acquainted with Von Dreber's woman down at the hotel. Ain't much goin' on in this town people don't see, Mulvane."

Mulvane nodded and smiled. He watched the woman coming toward him from across the room, then, a fairly tall, trim woman in her middle twenties, with dark brown hair and brown eyes. He watched her nod and joke with the men at the tables as she moved on, and he realized that he was seeing Miss Rosslyn Elder, proprietress of the El Dorado.

"Told Rosslyn you helped me git back here," Charlie was saying. "She's puttin' me up till I git back on my feet."

Miss Elder came up to the bar, looking Mulvane over casually with her fine brown eyes. Unlike most dance hall women, Rosslyn Elder did not dress the part. She wore an almost plain black dress with a string of pearls around her neck and no other ornaments.

"Mr. Mulvane," she said.

Mulvane nodded.

Rosslyn Elder said, "I understand Baudine and

some of his crew are in town this evening. If you'd like to keep out of the way until they're gone—"

She paused, watching the slow smile break out across Mulvane's face.

"Reckon I'll stay around for the fun," Mulvane said, and he heard Charlie O'Leary's low chuckle.

"He don't run," Charlie laughed, "not even fer Baudine or the devil, himself."

"Have a drink on the house," Miss Elder said, the interest in her eyes now. "May I ask your business?"

"Riding through," Mulvane said. "Figured I'd stop by and see Charlie on the way."

Rosslyn nodded and he knew what she was thinking. He was another drifter, a tough, who moved perhaps with the seasons, and who had no roots anywhere, and in a sense she was right. He'd been on the move for over ten years now since the nesters had killed his father. He'd been a stock detective, hired gun, part time deputy sheriff, along with many other things where a quick gun and a steady hand were required.

"Mulvane here has been havin' a little chit-chat with the Countess," Charlie was saying. "What'd she have to say?"

"Wants to run people like you into the ground," Mulvane told him, "and develop a super race."

Charlie stared at him. "Hells bells!" he muttered. "Allus figured the Dutchman was a queer one sittin' on top o' that hill. So he figures he'll take over the whole country from there?"

Mulvane smiled. "Reckon it's an experiment," he explained.

A flabby-faced man with round shoulders moved past them at the bar. He nodded to Rosslyn Elder, looked at Charlie O'Leary, and he gave Mulvane a quick curious glance with his mud-colored eyes.

Mulvane saw the silver star on his vest.

"Neil McAdams," Charlie O'Leary growled. "The law in this part o' the country, Mulvane, if you kin call it law."

"McAdams know you were burned out?" Mulvane asked him.

"He knows but he ain't sayin'," Charlie said grimly.

A small, thin-faced man now stepped up to Rosslyn Elder's side and said something to her in a low voice. She said immediately to Charlie O'Leary, "Baudine is outside, Charlie. Maybe you'd better go upstairs for a while."

"I ain't afraid—" Charlie started to say, but Miss Elder shook her head.

"I don't want any trouble here, Charlie," she told him. "Baudine has some of his toughs with him. You'd better go."

Charlie finished his drink and then stepped through a side door off the bar. Rosslyn said to

Mulvane, "How about you? They know you now."

The curiosity was in her eyes, and he felt that she was deliberately testing him, for reasons peculiar to herself. She wanted to see for herself what he was made of.

Mulvane turned and put both elbows back on the bar. Then he put the cigar in his mouth and tilted it toward the ceiling. He faced the door where the tough Varney Baudine would appear in a very short while, and he said softly, "You like them tough?"

"I like men," Rosslyn Elder smiled.

"Look at one," Mulvane said gently.

CHAPTER 3

Four men came in through the bat-wing doors, and the man in the lead was a tall, wiry fellow with opaque greenish eyes, a lean face, and hooked nose. On his right side he carried a Navy Colt in a black leather holster. He had peculiar pepper-colored hair.

"Baudine up front?" Mulvane asked Rosslyn Elder.

"He's dangerous," Rosslyn warned. "That's why I chased Charlie out. Baudine gets the job done."

"Not on me," Mulvane smiled.

Varney Baudine looked straight at Mulvane as he came across the room and he looked at Rosslyn Elder, also, a faint smile on his lean face. The three men with him scattered, one of them, a big fellow with a bull neck and a shock of straw-colored hair taking a position near the door. He stood there with his powerful arms hanging at his sides, a rather vacant expression on his wide face as he watched Mulvane at the bar.

Miss Elder said, "There aren't too many strangers in this part of the country and you were seen at the hotel with Von Dreber's woman."

"They know me," Mulvane smiled.

He pushed away from the bar, then, Rosslyn

watching him, as he moved up to where Baudine had stepped up to the bar and was now pouring a drink from the bottle the bartender had set down before him.

Mulvane said easily, "Baudine?"

Varney Baudine turned to look at him. He was the same height as Mulvane but not as heavy in the shoulders. He had long, slender, almost womanish hands, and he wore a black, flat-crowned hat with a black leather vest.

Baudine had not expected this move on Mulvane's part, but there was no particular surprise in his eyes. He said casually, "Reckon I know you, mister."

"The name is Mulvane," Mulvane said, and now he saw the small surprise come into Baudine's green eyes.

"Heard of you," Baudine nodded. "Say you're a big one across the mountains. I'll remember you."

"You'll remember, too," Mulvane said evenly, "that I'm a friend of Charlie O'Leary's."

"I won't forget that, either," Baudine smiled.

Mulvane turned away from him, then, heading toward the door because here it was evidently to begin. The big fellow with the blond hair now shifted his position so that he was partly blocking the doorway as Mulvane came toward him.

The big fellow had baby blue eyes the color of cornflowers, and a rather loose mouth, the lower jaw sagging. He was at least six feet, three inches tall, and he weighed well over two hundred pounds. Looking at him, Mulvane knew that he did not have a chance with this man as far as sheer strength was concerned.

Walking toward the door, Mulvane noticed that Neil McAdams was no longer in the room, and he wondered if McAdams was deliberately absenting himself, knowing that some of Von Dreber's hardcases were going to work on a man.

One of the other Baudine men who had come in with Von Dreber's ramrod had sat down at a table nearby, but he was getting up now, watching Mulvane, wiping his mouth with the back of his sleeve as he did so.

Mulvane pulled up in front of the big fellow. He said gently, "Step over, Jack."

He could have tried to squeeze past the man but he wasn't going to. The Baudine man just looked at him and then his eyes flicked in the direction of Baudine at the bar, and then moved toward the second man who was now coming toward them. He shook his head, and then Mulvane, smiling affably, but with his feet firmly planted on the wood floor, swung his right fist with all his might into the big fellow's stomach.

He could hear the wind leave the man in one big "whoosh." Mouth open, gagging for air, his blue eyes suddenly wild, the Baudine man bent over double, and as he did so Mulvane slipped the Colt gun from the holster and brought the barrel down across his skull, dropping him to the floor.

The second fellow was leaping toward him when he swung around like a cat, lining the gun on the man's stomach. He said softly, "You in it?"

The second man was shorter, a tough, freckled face, narrow green eyes. He had red hair and a pointed chin.

"You in it?" Mulvane repeated.

"Not anymore," the redhead grinned. "Not for now."

He rubbed his hands on his pants and looked at the gun as steady as a rock in Mulvane's hand. He moved back to his table, still grinning.

Holstering the gun Mulvane walked back to where Baudine was standing, a glass in his hand, elbows on the bar, watching. Baudine was smiling faintly, but the appreciation was in his eyes.

"The next time, Baudine," Mulvane said, "try it yourself."

"I might do that," Baudine nodded.

Mulvane saw Rosslyn Elder watching him from the other end of the bar, a thoughtful expression on her face. She seemed quite satisfied with what she'd seen.

He walked down to her and he said, "I'm obliged for the offer of help."

"But you don't need any help," Rosslyn said. "Is that it?"

"Always played it alone," Mulvane assured her.

"Not against a crowd like this," Rosslyn told him quietly. "This is different. We've never seen one like Von Dreber before. You know how he thinks; you know what he'll do."

Mulvane looked at the big fellow sprawled near the door and he said, "There's one of them didn't do much."

"I'd still walk easy if I were you," Rosslyn said, the warmth in her eyes now. She touched his arm and then she put her hand down as if ashamed.

It stirred him because it had been a long time since he'd run across a woman like this. He looked down at her and he knew that he had a haven here at the El Dorado, just like Charlie O'Leary, if he so desired.

"Passing on through?" she asked.

"We'll see," he said.

"You could help these small ranchers," Rosslyn told him. "Von Dreber has put the fear into the big cattlemen in this country, and they now support him because they're greedy and they want to squeeze out the little man anyway. They'll follow his lead just the way they did up at O'Leary's place this afternoon."

"Why should I risk a bullet in the back," Mulvane smiled, "for men I don't know?"

"What about O'Leary?"

"Friend of mine," Mulvane said. "Anybody else wants my gun pays for it."

Rosslyn looked at him steadily. "How much?" she asked.

Mulvane frowned. "You're not putting up the money?" he asked.

"Why not?" she smiled. "Somebody has to stop this man. His kind will overrun the country if he's not stopped."

Mulvane watched two Baudine men carry the still unconscious blond fellow out through the doors.

"The smaller ranchers are willing to fight if they have somebody to lead them," Rosslyn told him. "They're not afraid of Von Dreber, but they need a top gun to go before them. Please think about it."

"I'll think about it," Mulvane promised.

Looking at this fine-looking woman with the quiet brown eyes, he told himself that he would be a fool to ride away from here immediately.

Leaving the El Dorado, he headed back in the direction of the hotel and as he approached the building he saw some of Hilda Hannau's servants carrying her luggage out to the buckboard. Von Dreber, himself, came out through the door with the Countess, and he assisted her up to the seat, stepping up beside her.

Mulvane reached the hotel just as the stocky little Prussian, who was undoubtedly Von Dreber's valet, came out. The short man stared at Mulvane for a moment, and then recognizing him he started to splutter in German, running up to the buckboard and gesticulating with his hands, pointing in Mulvane's direction.

Mulvane turned to watch. The Countess had seen him, also, and she nodded now. Von Dreber sat up on the seat, the whip in his hand, listening to the valet, staring at Mulvane, his heavy jaw beginning to jut out.

Von Dreber said in excellent English, "You are the man who helped the rustler escape this afternoon?"

Mulvane pushed back his black, flat-crowned hat. "I'm the man," he nodded.

From the buckboard seat Von Dreber raised the whip to slash it down across Mulvane's face, but he stopped when he looked into the muzzle of Mulvane's Colt .44.

"Don't do it," Mulvane told him gently. "In this country, Von Dreber, don't come at a man with a whip. Come with a gun and come prepared to die."

Von Dreber lowered the whip. He said in a low, harsh voice, "We shall see you again, my friend."

The Countess Hannau was looking down at Mulvane, also, a faint smile on her face. The little Prussian was still mumbling in German as he put the last few pieces of luggage in the back of the buckboard and then climbed on himself.

The buckboard moved away, Von Dreber not even bothering to look at Mulvane again, a square figure of a man, head erect, shoulders stiff, and watching him Mulvane realized that he'd made an enemy who would never in this world forget an affront.

Stepping into the hotel, Mulvane was about to go up to his room when he caught a glimpse of Neil McAdams in the hotel bar off the lobby. McAdams was drinking alone.

Grinning, Mulvane crossed the lobby and stepped into the bar, pulling up next to McAdams. He said, "Sheriff, reckon I'd like to make a complaint."

McAdams turned to stare at him, a frown coming to his flabby face. "Complaint about what?" he growled.

"Some toughs tried to jump me in the El Dorado," Mulvane said. "Reckon I'd like to bring charges and have you arrest them, Sheriff."

"Hell," McAdams snapped. "I don't arrest anybody for a little scuffle."

"Then I'd like to make a charge against Von Dreber," Mulvane went on easily. "I saw him up at Charlie O'Leary's place this afternoon before they burned Charlie out."

McAdams rubbed his chubby hands on his vest, the scowl on his face. He said, "Anybody else see Von Dreber besides yourself?"

"I saw him," Mulvane said.

McAdams said slowly, "Any damned drifter who comes in here with a story like that is liable to end up with a bullet between the eyes. Now I'll tell you another story. The story is that O'Leary has been taking stock for years which didn't belong to him. If some of the ranchers in this country got together and tried to put fear into him maybe that's their business. Besides, you got no proof. It's your word."

"That the way you want it?" Mulvane asked him.

"I don't stick my neck out every time somebody squeals," McAdams snapped.

"You don't stick your neck out," Mulvane smiled, "until Von Dreber tells you to. That right, McAdams?"

The sheriff of Wickburg stared at him, hatred in his muddied eyes. "You're riding high," he said softly. "Watch out that you don't take a fall, Jack." He pushed away from the bar and went out into the street.

Mulvane went back into the lobby and then to his room. Even though the night was still young he'd been in the saddle since before dawn coming across the mountains, and he'd had a hard day and was tired.

Before retiring, however, he took his gun apart, cleaned it and oiled it, and was reassembling it when he heard the light knock on the door.

"Message for you, Mr. Mulvane," the desk clerk called through the door.

Mulvane opened the door and accepted the slip of paper the clerk handed to him.

"Boy brought it in from the street," the clerk said. "Said it was important."

Mulvane closed the door and opened the note. It was scrawled in pencil and signed *Charlie O'Leary*. It asked Mulvane to meet him down by the Big Wyoming Corral at the west end of town.

"Pullin' out tonight," Charlie had written. "Like to see you afore I go."

Mulvane stared at the piece of paper in his hand, and then he finished assembling the gun, buckled it on, and stepped toward the door. Charlie O'Leary may have suddenly decided to leave Wickburg and wanted to see him privately before he left, and on the other hand O'Leary might not know anything about the note, which would be a ruse to get Mulvane out in the open where Baudine's crew could work on him.

One way or the other, Mulvane intended to find out. If the note was authentic, and Charlie was in trouble, planning on a quick getaway tonight he, Mulvane, could never forgive himself for not showing up.

There was one way of finding out if Charlie was down at the Big Wyoming Corral. Charlie was staying at the El Dorado, and Rosslyn would know if he had planned on leaving.

Leaving the hotel, Mulvane headed up to the El Dorado. Pausing at the door, he looked for Baudine and Baudine's crew but did not see any of them. Rosslyn was not on the main floor, either, and when Mulvane inquired where she was he saw her coming down from the second-floor gambling room.

Rosslyn greeted him in surprise at the foot of the stairs.

"Charlie still here?" Mulvane asked.

Rosslyn looked at him curiously. "Charlie just received a note from you to meet him at the Big Wyoming Corral." When Mulvane's mouth tightened she said quickly, "Is anything wrong?"

"I have a note to meet him there," he said grimly. "We're being set up."

As he turned to go Rosslyn called after him, "Be careful."

Mulvane looked at her. "I'll come back," he said, and he saw the smile come to her face.

CHAPTER 4

Out on the street Mulvane turned right and headed down along the walk, moving quite fast now, hoping that he wouldn't be too late. He'd heard no gunshots as yet.

Coming into Wickburg late that afternoon he'd noticed the Big Wyoming Corral at the far end of town. It was the last building on the street, an ideal place for Baudine and his crew to set up an ambush.

As he passed the last house, Mulvane broke into a run, drawing his gun as he did so. He was moving past the pole corral toward the archway which led to the stable when he heard Charlie O'Leary call softly, "Mulvane!"

Mulvane pulled up quickly and as he turned around a gun boomed from the stable. He saw the red-orange wink of the pistol in the darkened entrance way, and he heard the lead slash into the corral post nearby.

He dropped down flat on the ground as two other guns opened up on him, and then Charlie's pistol boomed, also. Gun in hand, Mulvane crawled rapidly up against the corral fence behind which Charlie O'Leary was concealed.

"Had us set up," Charlie growled from the other side of the pole fence. "Damn near walked right into it. Figured I'd have a look first. Reckon you didn't send that note, Mulvane?"

"And you didn't send one to me," Mulvane told him.

He saw a shadowy form run along the wall of the stable, and then disappear around the corner.

"Baudine's bunch," Charlie said. "Hell of a thing to throw down on a man from a dark corner."

"Keep throwing it back," Mulvane told him. "I'll go around to the rear of the stable."

"Four-five of 'em there," Charlie warned. "Keep your head down." He fired his pistol through the pole corral and then he rolled to his left as an answering bullet came back.

Mulvane worked his way around the corral in the direction of the stable. Again a gun roared from the darkened interior of the stable, and then a second gun opened up from an abandoned building across the road where one of the ambushers had taken a position.

Reaching the far side of the corral, Mulvane flattened himself on his stomach and crawled toward the stable. He was within ten feet of the stable door when one of the men inside suddenly darted out, running low, heading for the corner of the corral around which Mulvane had just come.

He came straight toward Mulvane, not seeing him on the ground, and he was coming so fast that Mulvane did not even have time to raise his gun. Instead, he rolled his body hard up against the runner's legs, tripping him up so that he went down heavily, cursing as he fell.

Mulvane rolled, coming up on one elbow, gun steady in his hand. The Baudine man who had come out of the stable was up on his knees now, and he fired hastily at Mulvane at a distance of eight feet.

Mulvane felt the breath of the lead on his right cheek and he fired, knocking the man backward. He fell with a great shout and he lay still, arms and legs spread.

Leaping to his feet, Mulvane lunged toward the protecting wall of the stable as Charlie O'Leary opened up with his sixgun from the corral, keeping the gunmen inside the stable busy.

"Give 'em hell!" Charlie yelped.

Moving back to the corner of the stable, Mulvane circled it and then started on a run toward the rear of the long, shed-like building. He remembered that one of the men inside had swung around the opposite corner of the stable to take a position there.

As far as Mulvane knew now, there were still two men inside the stable, one at the corner of the building, and the fourth across the road in the abandoned building.

He had intended to round the stable and come up on the gunman at the corner but when he reached the rear of the building he noticed that the door was open. Instead of going around the building he stepped inside now, hearing the restless stamp of horses in the stalls. There were no lights in the stable, the ambushers having extinguished any lanterns which may have been burning.

Carefully, Mulvane moved down the long corridor toward the dim light of the open stable door at the far end. He was about halfway to the front when he heard a man come running in through the door behind him. He stepped quickly into one of the stalls, feeling his way in beside the horse tied there, rubbing the animal's flank gently.

He stood there as the runner hurried past him to join the two men up front. Outside the stable he could hear Charlie and the gunman from across the road exchanging shots.

As he waited in the stall the three men up front came back in his direction. They went by only a few feet away and he could see their figures dimly.

When they left by the rear door he stepped out of the stall and followed them. When he reached the rear exit he caught a glimpse of three men half-running toward an alley which opened up on the main street. They had evidently decided to pull out, leaving the fourth man still in his position across the road.

He headed back up toward the front of the stable and paused, gun in hand, keeping back in the shadows. Then he called out sharply, "Charlie. Hold your fire. I'm in here."

"One left," Charlie yelled, and then Mulvane saw his gun flash again.

The man who had been across the road fired back, but when Mulvane opened up on him he left his place of concealment at the corner of the abandoned building and sprinted up the street toward the town.

There was a possibility Mulvane could have put a bullet in his back as he ran but he held his fire, not relishing the idea of shooting a man in the back.

Charlie O'Leary came out from behind the corral fence, grinning, and said, "We put 'em on the run, Mulvane. See you got one of 'em."

Mulvane walked over in the direction of the man he'd shot, and then he bent down, striking a match, looking down into the face of the dead man. He was a gaunt, long-jawed fellow with a black mustache and a mole on the left cheek.

"Know him?" Mulvane asked.

Charlie shook his head. "The Dutchman has fifteen-twenty hardcase riders back on his hill. Reckon I don't know all of 'em."

They noticed that now that the shooting had stopped a few men were hurrying down from the center of town. Mulvane saw the bulky form of Neil McAdams up front.

McAdams came up as Mulvane was making a smoke and he said, "Who the hell is this?"

Mulvane said, "Reckon you're late, Sheriff."

"Five of 'em had us in a bind," Charlie O'Leary growled. "We got one of 'em."

McAdams said thinly, "I only see one dead man here, somebody you two might have jumped."

"That the way you figure it?" Mulvane asked him.

"I can figure it any damned way I please," McAdams told him.

"Then you should do something about it," Mulvane smiled. "You should try taking me in, McAdams."

Neil McAdams didn't say anything right away, and then he said gruffly, "I'll be asking a hell of a lot of questions around here until I find out who this hombre is."

"I'll tell you," Charlie offered. "He's one o' Baudine's boys, an' where in hell is Baudine?"

"Baudine ain't in town," McAdams snapped, and he bent down to have a look at the dead man.

As Mulvane and Charlie walked back toward the hotel Charlie said thoughtfully, "Came pretty damn close to gettin' us that time, Mulvane. Reckon you got yourself into a peck o' trouble when you helped me this afternoon. Best thing for you now is to ride the hell out o' here. It ain't your fight."

"You going to fight them alone?" Mulvane asked him.

"I ain't runnin'," O'Leary said stubbornly. "Still own that range even though they burned me out. Figure I'll be back on it afore long."

"Might bury you on it," Mulvane observed.

"An' I'll take some of 'em with me," Charlie growled.

Rosslyn Elder was waiting for them out on the porch of the El Dorado as they came up. She said to Mulvane, "You're still alive."

"I'm hard to kill," Mulvane grinned. "The next time Charlie sends any love notes he'd better send them to his best girl."

"Reckon I'll do that," Charlie laughed. He said to Rosslyn, "Baudine been around?"

"He left right after you received the note," Rosslyn told him.

"An' he was in on it," Charlie said tersely. "Maybe not down by that damned stable, himself, but he rigged it up, an' the next time he shows in this town, Rosslyn, I don't go in hidin'."

Rosslyn Elder just shook her head as little Charlie walked on past her and into the bar. She said to Mulvane, "He won't live too long that way."

"Reckon he's on the prod," Mulvane said. "They've been pushing him hard."

"Have you considered my offer?" Rosslyn asked him. "You're in this now whether you like it or not. If you shot down one of Von Dreber's riders you'll never be permitted to ride out of here." When he didn't say anything she went on casually, "My girl is making coffee upstairs. Would you like to join me and discuss it again?"

"Reckon I can stand the coffee," Mulvane nodded.

"What about the company?"

Mulvane looked at her. She was smiling at him in the shadows on the porch. He said, "I've met two beautiful women tonight."

"And one is spoken for," Rosslyn laughed. "Come along."

Mulvane followed her back into the gambling hall and then up the stairs to the main gambling rooms, which he found were luxuriously furnished for a western cattle town—red carpeting on the floor, mahogany tables. The big room was crowded, with waiters moving around the tables serving liquor.

He followed Rosslyn Elder down a corridor which opened on another door into her apartment, and they found a colored girl making coffee in a small kitchen in the suite.

The three rooms were tastefully furnished with mohair sofas and chairs, rich carpets and drapes, and expensive lamps. Mulvane said, "Reckon you've done well in this town. You weren't here when I passed through the last time."

Rosslyn poured the coffee when the colored girl left. She said as she sat down across from him at the tiny table in the kitchen, "I had a place in Grand Junction. When the town died I moved everything I had to Wickburg. Business has been good."

He watched her stir the coffee with a spoon and said, "You don't look like a gambling house woman."

"My father was in the business," she explained. "I worked with him and then I took over in Grand Junction when he died. My games are all straight and my liquor is good. That helps in this business."

Mulvane sipped his coffee. "The men bother you?" he asked.

He saw the smile come to her face. "Sometimes the wrong ones," she grinned. "I have some pretty good housemen in my employ, usually, and they don't try it twice."

When she got up to reach for the coffee pot on the stove and refill his cup, Mulvane reached for her arm. He said, "What if the right one bothers you?"

"Try it," the woman challenged.

He stood up and kissed her. He held her tightly, feeling her respond, feeling her hands on his shoulders, and then he raised his head and said, "We came here to talk business."

She looked at him steadily, her eyes wide and

deep and brown. "This is business," she said. "There aren't too many real men in this town."

He kissed her again, and then he permitted her to pour the coffee. She said without looking at him, "You still riding on now?"

"A smart man would be a damned fool to ride on," Mulvane laughed. He added, "I'm not signing on for your money, though. We'll figure it that I'm still a friend of Charlie's."

"Charlie O'Leary is going back to his spread," Rosslyn stated. "I'm staking him. He's going to run stock on his land. If you go with him it means that somebody is at last fighting Von Dreber. It'll give heart to the others." She added quietly, "It'll bring Von Dreber down on your neck, too, but I suppose you know that."

"Reckon I know it," Mulvane nodded. "Had big men on my neck before."

He finished his coffee and stood up, and Rosslyn Elder said to him softly, "I'm glad you're staying, Mulvane." She came over to stand beside him and then she put her arms around his neck and kissed him again. "Wickburg is a nice town," she said. "You'll like it here. A man can't drift forever."

Mulvane considered that fact. He'd been moving around for a long time now, always curious to see what was beyond the next hill, and having satisfied his curiosity he must go on again. This was his nature and he did not think that he would change—not even for the beautiful Rosslyn Elder who had much to offer, but who would find only unhappiness with him. He said almost sadly, "Reckon we'll see."

CHAPTER 5

In the morning when Mulvane stepped around to the stable to check on the claybank gelding, he found Charlie O'Leary saddling a small blue roan. The little rancher's jaw was tight and there was hardness in his pale blue eyes as he yanked on the cinch strap.

"Riding?" Mulvane asked.

"To hell back where I belong," Charlie scowled. "My own range."

Mulvane looked at the Winchester rifle protruding from the saddle holster and he said thoughtfully, "Reckon you're loaded for bear, Charlie."

"Maybe Dutch bear," Charlie said tersely, "if that Prussian shows his face on my range without fifty gunhands ridin' on his tail."

Mulvane signaled for the stable boy to bring out the claybank, and then he rolled a cigarette and watched the little rancher.

Charlie said, "You—you ridin' on, Mulvane?"

"With you," Mulvane told him. "Figured I'd like to see what they left of your place."

Charlie frowned at him. "Ain't no call fer you to stick with this thing," he said. "Not a dollar o' your money or a foot o' your range involved here, an' you were nearly set up last night on my account."

Mulvane said gently, "Nobody tells me where I can ride, Charlie. Reckon you know that."

Charlie O'Leary shrugged, and a few minutes later they rode out of Wickburg. It was a little past nine in the morning with the heat coming to the sun, burning the mists off the distant hills.

They rode due west, Charlie with his shoulders hunched, having very little to say as he sat in the saddle. Mulvane remembered this land from previous visits. It was good grazing land, possibly the best in the territory, and it was understandable that Von Dreber would try to set up his colony here.

As Charlie was making up a smoke Mulvane said to him, humor in his voice, "You ever hear of Friedrich Wilhelm Nietzsche, Charlie?"

The little rancher stared at him. "Who in hell is that?" he asked, "another damned Dutchman Von Dreber is bringin' in?"

Mulvane smiled. "You might say in a way," he explained, "that because of Nietzsche Von Dreber is here. Nietzsche is a philosopher. He has some ideas about setting up a super race."

Charlie O'Leary's mouth opened. "So that's what Von Dreber thinks he is," he said softly, "ridin' around on that white-faced black an' steppin' on people who get in his way. Super race or not, there's one thing I know about Von Dreber."

"What's that?" Mulvane asked.

"You put a bullet in his belly," Charlie said, "an' he goes down as quick as the next one."

Charlie's spread lay about six miles west and a trifle north of the stage road, and at mid-morning Mulvane sat astride the claybank gelding looking down at the still-smoldering remains of the burned-out shack.

"Damned lucky fer me I had that tunnel," Charlie growled, "or I'd o' been in there."

He dismounted and poked around in the burned embers with a long pole, pulling out a fire-blackened coffee pot which he stared at ruefully.

"This pot made the best damned coffee in the territory," he said. "I owe Von Dreber one fer that."

As he spoke Mulvane saw two riders coming up over the brow of a hill less than a quarter of a mile away, and even at the distance he recognized Von Dreber's big black with the white face.

The second horse was a buckskin, and seeing it, O'Leary said immediately, "Baudine, an' the devil himself."

Mulvane sat astride the claybank, leaning forward slightly in the saddle, arms folded across his chest as he waited for the two riders to come up.

"Likely comin' over to make sure they burned every damned thing," Charlie O'Leary growled. "If they want to make a play I'm takin' 'em on now, Mulvane."

Mulvane smiled faintly and said nothing.

The two riders came on at a slow jog, Von Dreber riding a few feet ahead, tall and square in the saddle, right hand stiff at his side. Mulvane had a better look at the big black now as they came up closer. The stallion was a magnificent animal, slightly bigger than his own claybank, and with speed lines in the legs and the chest.

Varney Baudine, a cold grin on his lean face, pushed back his black, flat-crowned hat as he rode up, revealing his pepper-colored hair. Von Dreber stared at Mulvane, dislike in his bleak blue eyes. When he spoke he spoke to Charlie O'Leary, though, and he said flatly with that very faint German accent, "You were warned to get out of this country. Why are you still here?"

"Because I belong here," Charlie snapped, "an' there ain't a man in these parts big enough to run me off."

"You're a cow thief," Von Dreber told him contemptuously, "and you'll hang from a tree before you're finished."

"Won't be your doin'," Charlie said slowly, "an' it won't be done by that fat-headed sheriff, neither. Reckon this is my range, Von Dreber, an' I'm stayin' here. I'm runnin' stock on this range, an' the next man tries to drive me off better wish he hadn't."

Varney Baudine spoke now for the first time. He looked down at the smoldering remains of

Charlie O'Leary's shack and said in a surprised voice, "You have a fire here, Charlie?"

The little rancher glared at him but before he could make any reply Mulvane said easily, "You still writing love notes, Baudine?"

Baudine's opaque gray eyes flicked. "What in hell does that mean?" he asked.

"Some dog sent me a note last night," Mulvane told him, "and then tried to set me up down near the Big Wyoming Corral."

Baudine smiled insolently. "Reckon you're kind o' shyin' at shadows, Mulvane," he said.

"Maybe so," Mulvane nodded, "but I've been set up twice in this town, already, and I don't aim to be set up again. You write that note?"

"Never heard of any damned note," Baudine told him, unabashed.

"And you're a damned liar," Mulvane said softly, and then he stepped down from the saddle, Baudine watching, eyes narrowed.

Mulvane walked casually toward the man, no expression on his face.

"You lookin' for gun play?" Baudine asked, uncertainty in his voice.

"Not this time," Mulvane smiled, and then as Baudine tried to pull the buckskin back Mulvane reached up and grasped the reins, holding the horse steady.

"What in hell is this?" Baudine snapped.

"Charlie," Mulvane said over his shoulder,

"keep Mr. Von Dreber amused." He heard Charlie O'Leary's gun come out of the holster with a soft, leathery sound.

Seeing Charlie's gun come out into the open Baudine's right hand dropped to the Navy Colt on his hip. As his long fingers closed on the butt of the gun, however, Mulvane's left hand shot out, grasping Baudine by the wrist. Before Baudine could lift the gun Mulvane yanked hard, jerking Baudine from the saddle. He landed heavily in the dust, cursing.

He'd managed to yank the gun from the holster as he was falling, though, and the big Navy landed in the dirt a few feet away from him. He was lunging for the gun when Mulvane kicked him full in the face with his right boot.

Varney Baudine screamed as his nose was shattered from the blow. He was almost lifted from the ground, and he fell over on his left side, the blood pouring from the crunched nose and upper lip.

Calmly, with Von Dreber watching silently, Mulvane walked over to pick up the gun and toss it into the nearby creek. Then he unbuckled his gunbelt, draped it across his own saddle, and he said to Baudine, "Get up."

It was brutal and he knew it, and he knew Varney Baudine, also. He was remembering that Baudine had either waited for him last night in ambush with a pistol in his hand, or he'd arranged for other men to do that particular piece of dirty work for him. Baudine had to have the fear put into him.

"All right," Baudine sputtered. "All right."

He'd pulled a blue bandanna from his pocket and was holding it to his bloodied face as Mulvane walked toward him.

Von Dreber sat like a rock on his horse, no expression on his hard face as he watched Mulvane yank Baudine to his feet.

"You were looking for a fight last night in the El Dorado," Mulvane told him, "when you had your crew with you. Reckon you can try it now if you like."

He saw the terrible hatred in Varney Baudine's eyes, and he saw the fear, too. Baudine looked like a vicious mad dog. As Mulvane walked toward him he picked up a heavy stone from the ground and hurled it at Mulvane's head.

Coolly, Mulvane ducked the stone, and then moved in fast, smashing Baudine full in the stomach with his fist. Baudine gasped as he spun around, and then he fell half on his side. He lay there, retching, agony in his face, blood still pouring from his battered nose.

Charlie O'Leary said, "Reckon he's had it, Mulvane."

Mulvane just nodded. He walked back to the claybank and strapped on his gunbelt, turning then to look at Von Dreber. The Prussian spoke for the first time since the fight had begun, contempt in his voice. He said a very strange thing, nodding toward the battered Baudine on the ground. He said calmly, "Shoot him. He's of no value."

"Shoot him, yourself," Mulvane said. "He's your boy."

Then he swung up into the saddle with Von Dreber still watching him, grudging respect coming to his face.

"I can use you," Von Dreber said. "The pay is very high."

Mulvane shook his head. "He's your kind," he said, nodding toward Baudine on the ground, and then he turned the claybank and started to ride off, Charlie following him.

When they were about fifty yards from the burned-out shack Mulvane glanced back and he saw Von Dreber riding in the opposite direction. Baudine still groveled on the ground but Von Dreber had let him lie there, making no attempt to help him.

Charlie O'Leary said, "You figure Von Dreber is finished with Baudine?"

Mulvane shrugged. "He'll have to bring in a bigger man," he said. "Baudine wasn't big enough."

On the way back to Wickburg Mulvane said, "Miss Elder tells me she's backing up your play, Charlie, staking you to more stock if you've got the guts to run it on this range."

Charlie nodded. "Told her this mornin' I'm pickin' up a hundred head from Sam Holloway over on Moose River. Sam's scared an' he's pullin' out."

Mulvane nodded. "How many men around here would back your play against Von Dreber?" he asked.

Charlie looked at him, screwed up his face, and then said, "Maybe half a dozen small ranchers like myself hate Von Dreber's guts enough to fight him if they have one big gun to lead 'em."

"I'm the gun," Mulvane said.

"That right," Charlie O'Leary said reflectively.

Mulvane was looking over the range as they rode along, noting the condition of the grass, and the dark line of willows which followed the course of the creek angling east and west.

"Good grass here, Charlie," he said, "and plenty of water. Your boys would be smart if they pooled their stock over here for the time being. You try to work it alone and Von Dreber will pick you off one by one, always on the charges that you're rustling his stock whether it's true or not."

"Makes sense," Charlie admitted. "Reckon I'll talk to some o' the boys. Them that are left."

"I understand Von Dreber has some of the big cattlemen on his side," Mulvane observed.

"Greedy sons-o-bitches," Charlie grated. "All of 'em are out fer all the range they kin get. The more small men they kin drive out the more range they pick up. They ain't seein', yet, that Von Dreber's takin' it all for himself."

"Who's the kingpin of the big ranchers?" Mulvane asked.

"Ed Grimes of Slash G," Charlie told him. "Other ranchers follow his lead when Ed lines up with Von Dreber. They figure they'll be in on the kill when the little fellers get it."

"Where's Slash G?" Mulvane asked.

"Two miles south," Charlie told him. "Ed runs near two thousand head o' stock." He stopped because Mulvane had pulled up the claybank and was looking toward the south.

"You go see your boys," Mulvane told him. "Get them to round up their stock and move them over to your range."

"Where you headin'?" Charlie asked in surprise.

"South," Mulvane said simply, and then he rode off, leaving Charlie O'Leary staring after him.

He rode due south over some of the most luxurious rangeland he'd ever seen, with the grass hock high and apparently with an abundance of water. The stock he saw, carrying the Slash G brand, were heavy with flesh.

A half-hour after leaving Charlie O'Leary he spotted wood smoke coming from the chimney of the Slash G ranchhouse less than a quarter of a mile away, and he headed in that direction.

Slash G was a big spread, lying along the north bank of a pebbly stream. A corral lay north of the main ranchhouse which was of logs and earth, and in the corral he saw a dozen fine Morgan horses. The bunkhouse for the Slash G riders was big enough to accommodate at least two dozen men. The ranchhouse was low, sprawling, with a stone chimney.

A man with an apron around his waist stood at the bunkhouse door as Mulvane crossed a meadow and rode straight toward the ranchhouse. Two men came out of the stable beyond the bunkhouse and were heading toward the corral. They slowed down, seeing Mulvane come into sight, and they watched him warily as he rode past. He recognized one of the men as the fellow whose horse he'd held at the fight at Charlie O'Leary's shack. He saw the recognition come into the man's eyes but he kept on riding, nodding to them slightly as he went by.

In front of the ranchhouse he dismounted, tied the claybank to the tie rack, and then stepped in under the wood awning. As he did so a square built, squat man with green eyes, and a heavy, blunt jaw came out into the open.

Looking at Mulvane carefully, he said, "All right, mister."

"Ed Grimes?" Mulvane asked.

The short man nodded. "Reckon I got plenty o' riders," he said.

Mulvane shook his head. "Friend of Charlie O'Leary's," he said, "I helped get him out of his shack, yesterday, where your crew had him pinned down."

Ed Grimes' green eyes flicked. He said softly, "You're damned cool about it, mister. Reckon you know you were helping a cattle rustler."

"Who were you helping?" Mulvane asked him.

Grimes stared at him. "For a stranger," he said grimly, "you got a hell of a lot of questions, mister. What brings you here?"

"Figured you'd like to know that Charlie O'Leary is putting stock on his range and he aims to keep it there."

"Whose stock?" Grimes asked sardonically. "Charlie's been runnin' other men's stock for years in this country."

"This stock he's buying," Mulvane smiled. "He's putting it on his range and nobody's running it off."

The short rancher said evenly, "That what you came to tell me?"

Mulvane nodded.

"And you're in with O'Leary? That the way it is?"

Again Mulvane nodded.

"And now you listen to me," Ed Grimes said softly. "You're a no-good drifter coming in here with a big gun and a bigger mouth, and they'll be taking you out with a hole in the head if you don't ride careful. O'Leary's a thief and we're ridding the country of him and his kind. You get in the way and you'll go with him."

Mulvane said, "The next time you come for Charlie you'll have more than one gun against you. Remember that, Grimes."

He turned and walked back to the tie rack and said as he was untying the claybank, "How long do you think you'll last, Grimes, after Von Dreber drives out the little men? You figure he'll stop there?"

He saw the anger come to Grimes' heavy face. "I'll worry about Von Dreber," he snapped.

"And I'll worry about O'Leary," Mulvane told him and swung into the saddle.

CHAPTER 6

Mulvane didn't ride very far after leaving the ranchhouse. The two Slash G riders who'd watched him come across the meadow moved out in front of him as he was swinging past the corral. The fellow whose horse he'd taken, a tall, raw-boned man with reddish hair, reached up and grasped the bridle, stopping the claybank.

"You still holdin' horses, Jack?" the Slash G man asked tersely.

Mulvane smiled down at him. "Left yours at the hotel stable," he said. "Next time don't trust a stranger, friend."

"You're pretty damned cool about it," the tall fellow snapped. "What in hell makes you think I won't pull you out o' that saddle an' roll you around in the dirt a little bit."

Mulvane's smile broadened. He noticed that the second Slash G man, a shorter, barrel-chested fellow with Indian black hair, and probably Indian blood in him, had moved back a step or two, and he said to this man quietly, "You're not in it, friend. Remember that."

As the taller rider stepped toward him he slipped his right boot out of the stirrup, placed it against the Slash G man's chest and pushed hard, sending him staggering back a dozen feet.

The breed's black eyes narrowed as he watched and his right hand was close to the pearl-handled Colt gun on his hip, but he didn't pull it out.

"Pick up your mount any time you want him," Mulvane said to the redhead, "but don't pick a quarrel with me, mister, or you'll be deader than hell."

He rode off, then, leaving the two Slash G men staring after him. As he rode he was wondering how many more of the big ranchers would go down the line with Von Dreber if it came to a full-scale range war. Undoubtedly, the big ranchers had recognized Von Dreber as the big stick who was getting things done in this country, and who had quelled the law, or bought him out. They would stick with the Prussian as long as he was successful, but they would move out if the going got too rough and there seemed to be a chance of Von Dreber going under. Their strength lay in union against the small cattlemen whose grass they coveted, and they would maintain that union only as long as success rode with them.

He assumed, also, that every big spread now had a hired gun or two on its payroll, which meant that things could get pretty rough for Charlie and his band of two-bit ranchers. There was only one way to counter a threat like this, and that was with guns of like calibre, and it was a question of how much and how far Rosslyn Elder would go in backing the small men. He had his respect for the tall, brown-eyed woman who was bucking the most powerful organization ever set up in the territory.

Reaching the stage road again, Mulvane hesitated, and then instead of riding on back to town, crossed the road and moved north toward the distant hills where Von Dreber's swastika brand was established, according to Charlie O'Leary. It was there that Von Dreber had built his strange stone castle with his imported masons.

Curiosity running through him, Mulvane headed toward the hills, noticing as he rode that the grazing wasn't nearly as good here as it had been back at Charlie's place, or at Slash G. Having come in late Von Dreber had had to take what was left, but he wasn't standing pat with his hand.

Again he passed the stock as he rode, and he paused once to examine more closely the odd crossed-angles brand enclosed by a circle. He was grinning as he rode away from the first clump of cattle, thinking how easy it could have been for little Charlie to change that swastika brand if he so desired. O'Leary's brand was an O with an L in the middle. A man had only to do some blotting out of an angle or two and the swastika became an L!

It was nearly an hour after he crossed the stage road that he spotted the gray towers rising above a fortress-like structure atop a high hill in the distance. The entire building was of stone, square in shape with four turrets. It was two stories high, the lower floor forming a kind of wall.

Staring at the unnatural structure for this country, Mulvane was thinking that it was like Von Dreber. No other rancher built on a hill in Wyoming Territory, always seeking the protection of sheltered valleys. Apparently Von Dreber had built his stone castle on the highest hill so that he could look down on lesser men.

At a distance he could see men moving about near the bunkhouse and the corrals, but he went no closer, smoking a cigarette through as he had his look at the castle. He turned and rode back now, heading in the direction of Wickburg.

Coming up this way he'd noticed a small stream off to his right, and he cut back, heading toward this stream, intending to water the claybank. Turning the claybank down through the willows along the edge of the stream he saw a white horse standing on the gravelly bank, and a moment later he spotted the Countess Hilda Hannau perched out on a big boulder looking down into the clear running water, apparently watching the trout.

Hearing his horse come down the trail Hilda Hannau straightened up, a smile coming to her face as she recognized him.

"Herr Mulvane," she said as she came down off the rock.

Mulvane dismounted and led the claybank

down to the edge of the water to drink. He said, "Looking over the country?"

"I've never seen country like this," the Countess told him. "There is no end to it."

"Filling up fast enough," Mulvane observed dryly. "Looks big, but there's only so much grass for cattle."

He bent down to drink and when he'd straightened up he noticed that she'd come up closer, and was now standing within arm's reach of him. She was tall, well-formed, her eyes clear and blue, warm now, but he imagined that they could be as cold as ice.

"You do not raise cattle, yourself, Herr Mulvane?" she asked.

Mulvane shook his head.

"What is your business?" she wanted to know, curiosity in her voice.

Mulvane put his right hand on the butt of the Colt .44 on his hip, and said casually, "Some men are quicker with this than others, and they get paid for being quick."

The Countess smiled. "A mercenary," she laughed. "Colonel Von Dreber is hiring men like you but you will not work for him. I saw one of our men returning to the castle a short while ago. He had been badly beaten. Was it you, Herr Mulvane?"

Mulvane kicked a stone loose with the tip of his boot. "Your ramrod pushed me too hard," he observed, and he was surprised at Hilda Hannau's light, tinkling laugh.

"You did splendidly," she chuckled, and he was thinking that Varney Baudine had not been a pretty sight riding back to the stone castle with his battered, bloodied face, but yet the Countess Hannau had laughed!

"We do not have men like you in my country," she said. "You are different, Herr Mulvane. We have had mercenaries who fought for money but they did not fight alone. You are alone?"

"I ride alone," Mulvane nodded, and then Hilda Hannau put out her hand and touched his softly.

"It is not good to be alone," she said in a soft voice.

Mulvane looked down at her hand and said, "If Von Dreber saw us together he would have me shot, wouldn't he?"

Hilda Hannau shrugged. "Are you afraid?" she asked coolly.

Mulvane looked at her for a moment, and then he grasped her shoulders, seeing the surprise come to her eyes. Roughly, he pulled her toward him and kissed her hard, full on the lips. It was not an act of love. There was no affection in it, no emotion, no passion.

He was smiling at her as he stepped back, and he said softly, "That was for Von Dreber."

Countess Hannau was breathing a little faster than usual, and her eyes had a glitter to them.

"Someday," she said in her low, musical voice, "I shall have you horsewhipped, and then I shall make love to you."

Mulvane stepped into the saddle, touched the brim of his hat, smiled at her, and then rode off in the direction of Wickburg. One thing he knew as he rode. He'd never met a woman quite like the Countess Hilda Hannau. He knew that she could do exactly as she'd said, and not only that but it would give her pleasure!

Back in Wickburg, Mulvane had a late dinner in the hotel dining room and then headed up the street to the El Dorado. He hadn't met Charlie O'Leary as yet while in town, and he assumed that Charlie was still making his rounds of the small ranchers.

The El Dorado was nearly deserted when he stepped inside. Rosslyn Elder was with the cashier behind the counter. Spotting him coming in through the bat-wing doors, she nodded and smiled.

He sat down at a corner table and watched Rosslyn take a bottle and a glass from the shelf and cross the floor to put it down on the table in front of him. As he was pouring his drink she said thoughtfully, "Taking a look at the country?"

Mulvane nodded. "O'Leary's seeing all the small ranchers on the bench," he said. "We're trying to get them to throw in their stock together on Charlie's range. Then we'll see what Von Dreber will do."

"He'll go for you," Rosslyn told him.

Mulvane smiled and fingered the bottle. "Reason I'm here to see you," he said. "They're too strong for us."

Rosslyn looked at him across the bottle. "That means you'll need more guns. How many?"

"Six," Mulvane said. "Eight if we can get them."

"Get them," she said.

"It'll go high," Mulvane warned.

"I'm prepared to go high," Rosslyn smiled, and Mulvane frowned.

"What's in it for you?" he asked. "A range war like this can bleed you dry. You'll get nothing when it's over."

"Nor will you," she reminded him, "and you might run up against a lot of lead." She added then, "I'm in this because I won't see Von Dreber's kind take over this part of the country. It'll have to be stopped before they get control."

Mulvane nodded. "I'll have O'Leary pick up his men tonight," he said. "We're holing up at his place. We'll need supplies."

"I'll send a wagonload out," she said.

"More money," Mulvane told her, "and maybe you'll stop this crowd and maybe you won't."

Rosslyn Elder watched his face. "My business," she said, "is gambling. Don't worry about me."

"There's men might like to worry about you," Mulvane said, and she blushed prettily.

Charlie O'Leary came in that evening with the report that of the eight small ranchers in the vicinity, five of them were coming in with their stock in the morning, but there was still a question if they could hold out against Von Dreber.

"You saw how many guns he had around my shack," Charlie scowled. "There's only ten of us."

"There'll be more," Mulvane assured him, and then he explained how Rosslyn Elder was going to back their play with hired guns.

Charlie whistled softly. "Might turn out to be a real war, yet," he said. "Don't figure there's any other way to stop Von Dreber now, exceptin' with guns. He won't listen to talk an' there's no use cryin' to the law."

"Pick out your men," Mulvane told him. "Get them out to your place."

"Shouldn't be too hard," Charlie smiled. "Talk's been goin' all around this damned part o' the country that big money is bein' paid for fast guns. They're headed in this way like bees around the hive. Most of 'em will take anybody's money an' they'll shoot their best friend in the belly to get it." He paused and then he said suddenly, "Reckon you know Trasker Flynn is in town?"

Mulvane frowned. Flynn was a lone gun like himself with a reputation as big as his own. On a number of occasions he'd worked with Trasker Flynn with ranchmen who were having trouble with unscrupulous sheepherders. Flynn, he remembered from experience, was incredibly fast with a gun, and as cool as ice under fire. Unlike other drifters, Flynn would not have come here to see if there was money to be paid for his gun. Flynn would have come on assignment—which meant that he was Von Dreber's man.

"You know Trasker pretty well," Charlie was saying worriedly.

Mulvane nodded again, the slight frown still on his face. Not only did he know Trasker Flynn very well, but he'd always rather liked the man. They would be on different sides in this war.

"Find Flynn over in the Territorial Saloon," Charlie O'Leary said.

Mulvane nodded again. "You line up what men you can," he said, "and get them out to your place in the morning."

After O'Leary left Mulvane walked up the street to the Territorial Saloon which lay beyond the hotel in the opposite direction from the El Dorado. He found Flynn in a card game in one corner of the room. The gunman was rather small, trim, very neat, with a black mustache and dark brown eyes. He wore a black frock coat and a string tie. His hands were very small, in sharp contrast to the big Colt he wore under his coat.

There was an empty chair at the table and Mulvane stood behind it, looking down at Trasker Flynn, seeing the slow smile break across the small gunman's face. Flynn had even, white teeth beneath the black mustache, and in every way he was a fine-looking man.

There were three other men in the game, drifters by the looks of them, hardcase riders, who, unlike Trasker Flynn and Mulvane, himself, had let themselves go. The dollar sign was on their backs, and the blood lust was in their eyes.

Flynn said, "Sit in, friend."

He didn't indicate to the other men at the table that he was acquainted with Mulvane.

With his boot tip Mulvane moved the chair back and then slid into the seat. He signaled for a nearby waiter to bring him some chips and then he sat there, slightly hunched in the chair, watching the game, noting the curiosity in Trasker Flynn's brown eyes.

One of the men at the table, a big, sandy-haired fellow with hulking shoulders and bloodshot eyes, was evidently the heavy loser in this game, and a poor loser at that. Several times Mulvane heard him grumbling under his breath as he picked up poor cards.

Sitting with his back toward the wall, as was Trasker Flynn, Mulvane saw Neil McAdams come through the bat-wing doors. His muddied eyes moved over the room, pausing for a moment at the table where Mulvane sat, a grimace of dislike coming to his face.

The big sandy-haired fellow threw in his hand and said sourly, "Damned cards allus runnin' the wrong way like everything else."

Flynn said cheerily, "You don't live right, my friend."

The sandy-haired man, who evidently did not know Flynn as one of the slickest gun handlers in the West, stared across the table, eyes narrowed.

"Kind o' dealin' yourself some pretty good hands, ain't you, mister?" he asked.

Trasker Flynn had been shuffling the cards, his small, smooth hands manipulating the pasteboards deftly. Mulvane watched him stop for one brief moment and his brown eyes seemed to change color. Then he started to shuffle the deck again and the smile was back on his face.

"Would you like a fresh deck, my friend?" he asked softly.

"Hell with the deck," the sandy-haired man growled. "It's the man handlin' it I worry about."

Trasker Flynn gave him a pleasant smile, revealing those even white teeth. He dealt the cards, giving Mulvane a hand this time.

Mulvane drew two aces, added another one in the draw, and then won his first pot without too much difficulty, beating the sandy-haired fellow's two pair, kings high.

The big fellow said tersely, "Hell of a business. Invite your friend in, an' then give him a winning hand first crack out o' the box."

Flynn looked at the hardcase carefully across the table, his face expressionless now, but he didn't say anything. Mulvane said it for him. He said coolly, "You have a big mouth, my friend. You should be more careful how you use it."

The tough looked at him, seeing more in him than he'd been seeing in Trasker Flynn. He said dully, "I'm not gettin' on your back, mister."

"I might be on yours," Mulvane told him, "if you're saying I was passed a fat hand."

The sandy-haired man mumbled something to himself and then relapsed into silence again. He had a bottle at his elbow and he was drinking quite heavily while he played, always a foolish practice.

They played three more hands before the action came. Mulvane won another small pot with two pair, and on the third hand Flynn took in a fairly sizeable pot with three jacks.

Mulvane had been dealing when Flynn drew the jacks, and the sandy-haired man said thickly, "I'm out. This damned game is rigged."

Flynn's hands were flat on the table. He said evenly, "You have made several insinuations tonight, my friend, and I'm afraid I didn't like any one of them."

"An' to hell with you, too," the hardcase

growled. "I'm not takin' rough talk from a little tin-horn like you."

Flynn's brown eyes dropped to his hands on the table. Then he pulled his hands from the table and let them hang at his sides. His coat was open now, and beneath the coat the Colt gun hung clear. It had a pearl handle with a silver inlay. He said slowly, "Now you have a gun, my friend. Show it to me whenever you wish."

Immediately, the two other men at the table with him stood up and backed off. Mulvane sat where he was, making no move to go, watching the sandy-haired man out of the corner of his eyes.

The big fellow said tersely, "Two of you. I don't like them odds."

"I'm on your side," Mulvane smiled. "I don't want to see you killed."

The hardcase hesitated one moment, his eyes flicking in Mulvane's direction. When his right hand started to move Mulvane lifted his own sixgun and slapped the barrel across his hat. With a grunt the big fellow fell forward across the table, arms outstretched, knocking over his liquor bottle as he fell.

When Mulvane looked at Trasker Flynn he saw that Flynn's gun was out of the holster, and the muzzle of it had been lined straight and true on the big fellow's middle. In one more moment the hardcase would have been dead.

Mulvane said casually, "Buy you a drink."

Trasker Flynn holstered the gun, picked up his chips, nodded, and walked toward the bar. Neil McAdams said as they passed by him at the bar, "Still the tough one, are you?"

"Tougher than ever," Mulvane told him.

He waited as Flynn cashed his chips and then he called for a bottle.

"I'm obliged," Trasker Flynn smiled. "I didn't want to kill that fellow."

"Figured you didn't," Mulvane nodded. He poured two drinks and he said, "What brings you to Wickburg?"

Flynn lifted the glass to his lips, watching Mulvane in the mirror, and he said, "Work."

"You lined up?" Mulvane asked him.

Flynn nodded.

"Von Dreber?"

Flynn downed his drink and put the glass back on the bar. "Von Dreber," he admitted, and when Mulvane frowned, Trasker Flynn said regretfully, "That means you're on the other side this time."

Mulvane nodded. "Von Dreber's a bad one," he said.

Trasker Flynn smiled faintly. "Are any of them *good*," he asked in a soft voice, "when they pay money to men like us?"

"You know the story here?" Mulvane asked him.

"Old story," Flynn said. "Little coyote rustlers

eating away at the big men. The big men want it stopped and they don't want to dirty their hands. Nothing new about it."

"More than that," Mulvane said slowly, and then he told Trasker Flynn of his conversation with the Countess Hannau, Flynn listened without expression until Mulvane had finished.

"The small ranchers like O'Leary may have taken a beeve or two," Mulvane admitted, "but that's not the reason Von Dreber's running them out. He wants the whole damned range for himself, and he wants to bring his own kind of people in."

Flynn frowned and twirled the shot-glass around with his fingers. "Von Dreber struck me as a queer one," he admitted. "I never figured he'd be as bad as that. I don't like it."

"And you can't walk out of it," Mulvane said.

Flynn shook his head. "I took Von Dreber's dollar," he said. "Reckon that makes me part of his crew, at least for the time."

Mulvane knew how it was with the little gunman. The men who sold their guns for the high dollar had a warped sense of honor. He'd given his word that he'd fight for Von Dreber and now he would stay.

Back at the El Dorado Mulvane found Charlie O'Leary at the bar chatting with two lean, hard-faced men who'd apparently just come in off the trail, the dust still on them. They were unshaven, unkempt, except that the guns on their hips were in excellent condition, the black leather holsters well-oiled.

"Two boys I lined up," O'Leary smiled. "They're ridin' out with us in the morning."

Mulvane had his look at the two hired gunhands. They looked quite alike even though he was positive they were total strangers, having met at this bar but a few minutes before. They bore quite a startling resemblance to each other. One man was slightly taller than the other, sandy-haired, with bleak blue eyes and a nose broken across the bridge.

The second fellow had lighter hair, almost blond. He had the same pale blue eyes and straight mouth.

"What's your name?" Mulvane asked the sandy-haired fellow.

"Smith," the gunman grinned. "Bill Smith."

Mulvane grinned back. "Everybody in this damned country is named Smith," he said. Turning to the blond fellow he said, "What do they call you, Jack?"

"Smith," the blond man said soberly, "Joe Smith, only we ain't brothers."

Mulvane knew how it was with them. This breed didn't have names, or having them had given them up when the law put a price on their heads.

"We're running up against a tough crew,"

Mulvane said. "Reckon Charlie told you that. You could come out of this with a hole in the head."

Joe Smith scratched his neck and then he said, "You're in it, Mulvane, an' we heard of you. Reckon that's good enough for us."

Bill Smith nodded in agreement. Mulvane looked at them, and he said, "Ride out in the morning."

Joe Smith said hesitantly, "Reckon we could use a little shave money. Both of us just rode in an' we're flat broke."

Mulvane slipped each man a ten-dollar bill. He said, "You'll pay me back when you're paid off."

When the two hired guns had left Charlie O'Leary said, "I got three more lined up. That makes five in all." His round face became quite serious then, and he said slowly, "Didn't figure I was startin' a full-scale range war when I decided to buck Von Dreber. I was just mad—mad clean through."

Mulvane shrugged. "Somebody had to start it, Charlie," he observed. "Somebody always has to start it."

Charlie nodded. He rubbed his jaw and he said, "Reckon Trasker Flynn's lined up with Von Dreber, ain't he?"

Mulvane nodded.

Charlie frowned. "That part of it ain't good,"

he said. "Reckon you wouldn't want to stand up against Flynn now, would you?"

Mulvane shrugged. "We'll see," he said, and he said no more on the subject.

CHAPTER 7

In the morning Charlie O'Leary loaded up a wagon with supplies and rode out of town, Mulvane on the buckboard beside him, the claybank tied to the tailgate. Five men rode with them, and the spectacle caused plenty of comment in the streets of Wickburg.

Mulvane had seen Neil McAdams watching from the door of the sheriff's office as they drove by with the wagon, and many other townsmen and storekeepers watched them silently, knowing what was going on. For the first time someone was definitely opposing the swastika brand.

It was past nine o'clock in the morning when the outfit left Wickburg, and already the sun was heavy on the land. The five hardcase riders came on in the rear, swinging out wide to avoid the dust kicked up by the wheels.

"Good men," Mulvane observed, glancing back. "Not honest, but good."

"Good for what we need," Charlie laughed. "You figure Von Dreber will hit at us right away?"

"He can't afford to wait," Mulvane observed. "The longer you stay here the harder it will be for him to push the others out. He'll come with a good-sized crew to see how much of a fight we'll put up."

Charlie said tersely, "Them big ranchers like Ed Grimes got no use fer our kind, Mulvane. They'd like to see all of us six feet under pushin' up the grass. They're set an' that's the way they want it. Anybody tries to make a livin' runnin' a few head o' stock is just dirt under their boots."

It was high noon when they reached Charlie's burned-out shack and found the small ranchers already waiting for them with several hundred head of cattle grazing on a slope nearby. There were five ranchers and three of them had riders with them, making a total of eight. With the five Charlie had brought out there were fifteen altogether.

"We're here, Charlie," a rancher by the name of Ben Meigs growled. He was a short, heavy-set man with a blunt jaw and hard black eyes. "Which one is Mulvane?"

Charlie nodded toward Mulvane who'd stepped down from the wagon and was untying the claybank from the buckboard.

"Shake your hand," Ben Meigs said. "Hear you're usually with the big fellows cleanin' out rustlers."

"You a rustler?" Mulvane smiled.

"Hell," Ben Meigs grinned. "Only rustler hereabouts is Charlie O'Leary."

"Hell with you, too," Charlie laughed. "I hadn't

gotten you out here, Ben, an' Von Dreber would o' had his swastika brand on your backside afore sundown."

Mulvane said, "I saw a line shack coming out here. That yours, Charlie?"

"Mine," Charlie nodded.

"We can hole up there," Mulvane observed. "Some inside and some outside. We can graze the stock along the north side of the creek."

It was agreeable to the rest of the ranchers. Mulvane shook hands with all of them, making no effort to introduce the five hardcase riders they'd brought out from Wickburg. They were a breed apart. Their interest in this fight lay only in the dollars they would collect.

At the line shack Mulvane had a look inside, finding four bunks and a rusted stove.

"Ain't much," Charlie admitted.

They kicked together a wood fire on the outside of the shack, and soon had the coffee pot boiling away merrily. They sat around under the cottonwoods along the creek bank, smoking cigarettes, sipping the coffee.

After they'd eaten Mulvane sent four of them out with the herd, dividing the group into four watches.

"Von Dreber might come tonight," he told the men, "or he might not come for a week. We won't know until he's here, but we're going to be prepared."

Joe Smith said as he chewed on a twig, "Hear Trasker Flynn is with this crowd."

Mulvane looked at him. "That's right," he said.

"He's a bad one," Joe Smith observed.

"Afraid of him?" Mulvane asked.

"I ain't afraid of the devil, himself," Joe Smith said softly, and Mulvane could see that he meant it.

With the first guard set, Mulvane stepped into the saddle and made a two-mile-wide circuit around the line shack, finding nothing. The distant hills and ridges were bare, the grass waving gently in the light breeze.

As he was heading back, though, he saw a rider coming toward them from the direction of Wickburg. Ten minutes later he recognized Rosslyn Elder astride a chestnut mare. She looked different in riding clothes, very trim and cool in the fawn-colored pants and white blouse. She rode well.

"Everything all right?" she asked.

"We're holed up for a fight," Mulvane told her. Then he said thoughtfully, "Reckon Von Dreber knows you're the one who's backing Charlie O'Leary out here. He won't take that and forget about it."

Rosslyn shrugged. "Nobody makes war on a woman in this country," she smiled.

"Von Dreber is not from this country," Mulvane

observed. "Reckon I'd be careful. I wouldn't do too much riding around these hills alone."

Rosslyn patted the Winchester rifle in the saddle holster, and she said, "I know how to use this, Mulvane."

They rode on to the line shack and Rosslyn had a word with Charlie and the other ranchers, the five gunhands watching her speculatively. Bill Smith said to Mulvane in a low voice, "She the one payin' us?"

Mulvane nodded. "She's the one," he said.

"Hell," the sandy-haired gunman grinned. "A looker like that don't have to pay me no money. All she has to do is say the word."

Ben Meigs said as Mulvane came up to the group of ranchers, "How long you figure we ought to stay out here, Miss Elder?"

Rosslyn Elder looked at Mulvane, saying nothing, and he appreciated this. He said, "We'll wait till they come after us."

"What if they don't come?" Meigs asked bluntly. "What if Von Dreber stays up there on his damned hill an' lets us sweat it out?"

"He'll come," Mulvane assured him. "If he doesn't we'll go after him."

Now it was Charlie O'Leary's turn to stare. "Go after him?" he gulped.

Mulvane smiled. "You told me that bunch ran off your stock, Charlie," he said.

"They run it off," Charlie scowled. "Every

damned head. They're mixed in with Von Dreber's stock right now."

"Then we'll take a ride over there some day," Mulvane said, and he saw the two Smiths grinning at him appreciatively.

When Rosslyn Elder rode back later in the afternoon Mulvane accompanied her to the stage road. He said as he left her, "I'd kind of keep close to town from now on."

"I'll be all right," Rosslyn assured him. "Watch out for yourself."

She gave him a warm look and then she rode off.

At dusk Mulvane set his watch for the night, ordering the herders to move the stock in closer to the creek. He posted his guards on the surrounding hills and then had the remainder of the men turn in for the night.

It was an hour past midnight when the raiders struck. Mulvane, himself, had just come off guard duty and was spreading his tarpaulin outside the line shack when he heard the shots and the quick yells.

There was no moon tonight, but plenty of starlight, and even at a distance he could see the band of riders break out over a low ridge to the north and swing down toward the creek, splitting into two prongs as they rode. They were moving toward the grouped bunches of cattle along the creek.

Mulvane ran to the claybank which he'd tied nearby. As he swung himself into the saddle he heard Charlie O'Leary's high-pitched whoop. The two Smith riders who had been out with Mulvane had had their horses saddled, also, and the three of them rode down along the creek.

The raiders had already gotten the cattle moving and were heading them up along the creek in the opposite direction. There were at least twenty men behind the herd with many others moving in between the guards. On the far side of the herd Mulvane caught a glimpse of a big black with a white face, and a square-set man in the saddle. He tried to work the claybank through the milling stock toward Von Dreber but it was impossible.

Charlie O'Leary's guards, who'd come down off the near grade, opened fire on the raiders, but they were heavily outnumbered. As Joe Smith maneuvered his mount, trying to get the stock to mill and turn back on itself, Mulvane shouted to him, pointing to Von Dreber, indicating that Smith should try to make his way over in Von Dreber's direction.

A moment later, however, Joe Smith's mount was bowled over by the plunging cattle. The blond gunman leaped clear of the stirrups, landing on his feet like a cat, but he was on dangerous ground in the night with frightened stock all around him.

Mulvane rapidly worked the claybank in close

to him, giving him a hand up behind. As he tried to work his way out of the stock now he saw a rider with a strangely mottled white face fire a shot at them across the heads of the cattle. It was only later that he realized the man who fired the shot was Varney Baudine, his broken nose plastered with white tape to hold it in place.

He could hear Von Dreber's booming voice above the uproar as the raiders pushed off with the stock. The remaining men from Mulvane's crew at the line shack were now swinging into action, led by Ben Meigs, and they were driving a wedge through the moving cattle, separating them into two parts, and turning the larger section back toward the grazing grounds.

Mulvane dropped Joe Smith to the ground when he was clear of the stock, and then he worked in behind Meigs' riders as they split the herd. Fifty or more of the stock, however, were moving off at a very fast rate accompanied by some of Von Dreber's crew. One man seemed to wobble in the saddle as he rode.

Mulvane and Meigs managed to get the rest of the herd milling where they soon piled into the rear of the column and came to a frightened, bawling halt.

Charlie O'Leary rode up hard, yelling excitedly, "They're pullin' out!"

Mulvane watched the fleeing riders as they followed the stock they'd cut from the main herd.

"How many you figure there were, Charlie?" he asked.

"Forty-fifty," Charlie told him. "I winged one of 'em."

"Have anybody hurt?" Mulvane asked him.

"Tom Stacey," Charlie said. "Got a bullet in the arm, but it ain't bad. We—we goin' after 'em?"

"Not tonight," Mulvane told him. "There'll be another time."

He had only one-third as many guns as Von Dreber, and it would have been foolhardy to ride after them. They would accomplish very little if they caught up with them.

"Run 'em off, anyway," O'Leary growled. "You see Von Dreber in that crowd, Mulvane?"

"He was there," Mulvane nodded.

Back at the line shack they kicked up the fire and Tom Stacey, the wounded rider, sat on a blanket, cursing, as they cut away his shirt. The bullet had passed through the upper part of his arm, and after Mulvane had had a look at the wound he said to Charlie, "Have somebody take him into town to get that wound dressed. We won't have any more trouble tonight."

Ben Meigs said dismally, "Reckon they took damn near a hundred head, Mulvane. They come a few more times like that an' we'll have plenty o' rangeland but nothin' on it."

"Not that many," Mulvane told him as he put a temporary bandage on Stacey's arm. He stood up, then, and he said without looking at Meigs, "You figure you're better off on your own range, bucking them alone?"

Meigs shook his head. "Stickin'," he said.

Lars Cannivan, a small rancher, said quietly, "What I kin see, most o' the stock they got tonight was mine. We got any chance o' gettin' 'em back, Mulvane?"

Mulvane looked at the circle of grim-faced men in the firelight. "Tomorrow's another day, boys," he said quietly, and then he said to Charlie O'Leary, "How big a crew does Von Dreber have over at his place?"

"Maybe a dozen riders," Charlie said.

"We might visit Von Dreber in the morning," Mulvane told them. "That suit everybody?"

Joe Smith said, "Anybody's talkin' big now might keep some o' that big talk for tomorrow. You all savvy that?"

From their faces Mulvane could see that they savvied.

"Be good," Lars Cannivan growled, "to run the other way for a change."

In the morning a light rain was falling as they saddled up. Mulvane unrolled his slicker and buttoned it up around his neck, the men with him doing likewise. He'd decided not to take the entire crew over to Von Dreber's range, and he'd selected his five gunhands, along with Charlie

O'Leary. The remainder of the crew was to guard the stock.

They rode due north toward the misty hills with Charlie riding at Mulvane's side. Mulvane said to him once, "You know Lars Cannivan's brand?"

"C Cross," Charlie said promptly. "You figure they'll have this stolen stock on Von Dreber's range?"

Mulvane nodded. "Yours, too," he observed. "Swastika brand changed to Circle L."

Charlie grimaced. "Nothin' wrong, Mulvane," he protested, "takin' what belongs to me. Von Dreber's had his riders movin' over all this damned part o' the country pickin' up yearlings don't belong to him an' throwin' his brand on 'em. Nobody's had the guts to stop him."

They rode on into the mist and after a while O'Leary said thoughtfully, "You figure Trasker Flynn was with that bunch last night, Mulvane?"

Mulvane shook his head. "Not his kind of work," he said. "Flynn wouldn't sign for that. Baudine is still doing Von Dreber's dirty work. Flynn will be there with the big gun when they need him."

They passed clumps of cattle now, steaming in the misty rain, and the first groups all had the swastika brand. As they moved on, though, deeper into Von Dreber's range, riding somewhat west of the castle on the hill, they began to cut out little clumps of C Cross and Circle L stock, moving the cattle on ahead of them as they rode.

They did it deliberately, taking their time about it, picking up a few head here and a few head there. By mid-morning they'd cut out nearly fifty head before they ran into the first Von Dreber rider.

He came out of a line shack along a willowy creek, staring in surprise as the seven men moved by. He was spilling frying pan grease on the ground, but seeing them he went back quickly with the frying pan and came out with a rifle in his hands.

Mulvane moved away from his riders, heading straight toward the shack. The Von Dreber rider was the big fellow with the shock of yellow hair and the bull neck whom Baudine had set on Mulvane in the El Dorado his first night in town.

The Von Dreber crewman stared at the small bunch of stock moving past, his lower jaw drooping stupidly, and then he said, "Where in hell are you boys goin'?"

Mulvane said to him pleasantly, "You don't see Von Dreber's brand on this stock, do you? We're taking them back."

When the big fellow made a move to lift the rifle Mulvane said to him carefully, "You better use it if you cock that hammer. You'll be dead if you don't."

The big blond man put the rifle down again. He said tersely, "Mr. Von Dreber won't like this."

"Tell him to stop us," Mulvane said and he turned and rode back to his crew.

They continued on across Von Dreber's range, picking up more stock as they went, but keeping their little herd bunched.

Charlie O'Leary said, "That Jug Streiber will be ridin' up to see Von Dreber now."

"Let him," Mulvane said. "That's why we're here, Charlie."

"Maybe so," Charlie muttered. "Maybe so."

CHAPTER 8

It was nearly noon, and the rain had slackened to a very thin mist when five riders approached them from the east. Mulvane immediately recognized Von Dreber's big black in the lead.

Charlie O'Leary said, "Trouble."

Mulvane pulled up, the six men with him swinging back from the little herd they'd collected and forming a kind of crescent behind him. He sat there, waiting for Von Dreber to come up.

A small, slim man with black, flat-crowned hat, rode at Von Dreber's side. The small man was Trasker Flynn.

Varney Baudine, his broken nose covered with strips of dirtied plaster, rode slightly behind Von Dreber. He was astride his buckskin horse.

Von Dreber pulled up less than a dozen feet from Mulvane, staring at him steadily, his bleak blue eyes hard, jaw thrust out. A small vein on his left temple was pulsing rapidly.

"What are you doing on my range?" he snapped.

Mulvane glanced at Trasker Flynn sitting astride a small blue roan, arms folded across his chest, face expressionless. If Flynn knew him there was no recognition.

Baudine sat on his buckskin, hatred in his eyes as he stared at Mulvane. Mulvane said easily,

"Our combine lost some stock last night. Figure we'd come over here and have a look. We're cutting them out now."

Von Dreber's face turned almost purple with rage. Flynn's face was a mask, but Mulvane detected the slight humor in the little gunman's eyes.

"You will come on my range?" Von Dreber rasped.

"I'll come on your damned range any time I find our stock on it," Mulvane assured him. "We cut this bunch out and we're taking them back. We'll run every head past you to check the brand if you want, but don't try to stop us."

Von Dreber glanced at Flynn, and Trasker Flynn said casually, "Seven to our five, Mr. Von Dreber. They're not cowboys he's got behind him, either." He lifted his voice, then, and he said to Bill Smith, "I know you, mister."

"Do you?" Bill Smith smiled.

Mulvane said, "We're going by. Anybody wants trouble had better make it now."

He moved his horse, then, riding past Von Dreber so close that he could have reached out and touched the man with his hand. He could hear Von Dreber's breath come and go as he moved by.

The big Prussian cattle rancher said nothing, though. He sat astride the black horse, face flushed. "Someday," he said finally, "you'll die."

"Everybody dies," Mulvane said, and he kept riding, past Baudine on the outskirts of the group, and he gave Baudine a grim smile as he went by.

"You're pretty rough," Baudine said in a low voice, "for now. You might not always ride so high."

Mulvane's crew came on behind him with the stock they'd cut out. They rode at a leisurely pace, heading south again toward Charlie's range. Charlie said when they were a quarter of a mile away, "Nobody's crossed Von Dreber like that before, Mulvane. He'll remember you."

Mulvane nodded. "I'll remember him," he said.

They set a double guard around the stock, keeping them bunched and close to the creek again.

Ben Meigs said, "We got our stock back. What now?"

"One thing at a time," Mulvane smiled. "Von Dreber's been doing all the pushing. Now he's being pushed back. We'll watch him."

By mid-afternoon the rain was over and the sun began to push through. The men came out of their cramped quarters in the line shack and quickly got a fire going, drying their damp clothing.

It was dusk when they saw the red glow in the sky, some distance south and west of the shack. Charlie said slowly, "That'll be George Tibbs' place. Reckon he wishes he'd gone in with us now." To Mulvane he said, "Tibbs figured he'd stay where he was when I spoke to him."

Mulvane tossed away the cigarette he'd been smoking and said suddenly, "We'll have a look. Saddle up."

He took ten men with him, riding down to Tibbs' spread. When they arrived after dark, the log house was just falling in, sending a shower of sparks high into the sky.

The corral gate was wide open and empty. They found Tibbs, himself, sprawled on his face near the corral, his body riddled with bullets.

Charlie said grimly, "George got his warning just like I got mine, only I was lucky."

In the light from the smoldering log cabin Mulvane studied the hoof prints in the soft earth. He figured there had been at least twenty riders in the party which had hit at George Tibbs' little spread when he'd refused to pull out. He looked around at the circle of grim-faced men. He said softly, "Any of you boys figure you're safer fighting it out alone now?"

"We'll stick," Ben Meigs growled. "Gettin' to be a hell of a country, though when a bunch o' murderers can ride up an' shoot down a man like George who's never bothered anybody before."

"In McAdams' book," Charlie O'Leary observed, "George was changin' brands."

When they returned to the line shack they had a visitor who'd just come out from Wickburg, and was warming himself at the fire outside the shack. Mulvane recognized him immediately as one of the bartenders from Rosslyn Elder's establishment. He was a flabby-faced man with a thin layer of brown hair and a long mustache.

Mulvane said to him as he came up, "Miss Elder send you out?"

"Miss Elder didn't send me," the bartender scowled, "but we figured you'd want to know, anyway."

Mulvane looked at him. "What happened?" he asked.

"Somebody worked over Miss Elder with their fists tonight," the bartender said bitterly, "and they did a pretty damned good job of it."

Mulvane heard Charlie O'Leary start to curse in a low voice.

"Where the hell were your floormen?" Mulvane snapped. "I thought she had a tough crew down there."

The bartender shook his head. "Nobody heard anything," he said. "She was upstairs. The colored woman who works for her was out. Somebody got in there. That's all we know, mister."

"I'll ride back with you," Mulvane said, and when Charlie O'Leary started toward his horse he said, "Better stick with the stock tonight, Charlie. This may be a move to get us into town." He said to the bartender, "You say it happened early this evening?"

"Early," the bartender nodded. "Place was almost empty."

As Mulvane stepped back into the saddle, Joe Smith said casually, "Reckon I'd like to ride along, Mulvane. Can't stand a man works on a woman."

Mulvane nodded and the two of them rode beside the bartender as they left the camp. Joe Smith said as they rode, "Von Dreber was pretty riled up this morning when you crossed him, Mulvane. You figure he went in? Reckon he knows Miss Elder's backin' our play out here?"

Mulvane shook his head slowly. "They know she's backing us," he said, "but this could still be a personal thing."

Joe Smith looked at him, but Mulvane said no more on the subject. He did know that Varney Baudine hated him and would do anything in his power to get back at him. Possibly, this was Baudine's way of making him suffer. Baudine may have sensed that Mulvane was sweet on Rosslyn Elder, and he'd worked over the girl out of sheer spite.

It was past ten o'clock in the evening when they rode into Wickburg, tying up out in front of the El Dorado. As he stepped up on the porch the first man Mulvane saw was Neil McAdams coming out through the bat-wing doors. The flabby lawman had his hat pushed back on his head and there was a liquor shine to his face.

He said thickly, "You in town again, Mulvane?"

Mulvane pulled up in front of him, his face tight. He said, "You learn who worked over Miss Elder tonight?"

McAdams glared at him, dislike in his round face. He said, "She's been helpin' rustlers and drifters in this country for a long time. Maybe it's no damned business of mine what happened to her. She's asked for trouble."

Mulvane put out his right hand, shoving the palm hard into Neil McAdams' face, slamming the lawman back against the wall of the building. Partly dazed McAdams slid half way to the floor, and then a wild crazy anger came to his face. His right hand moved to the gun on his hip, but he wasn't nearly fast enough.

Joe Smith stepped forward, slamming him across the fingers with the barrel of his own six-gun. "You'd be dead," the blond gunman grinned, "before you had that hog-leg out of the holster. Put it down that I saved your life, Sheriff."

They walked into the El Dorado leaving McAdams wordless on the porch, holding his numbed fingers with his left hand. Joe Smith moved toward the bar and Mulvane went up the stairs to the second-floor gambling rooms and then down the corridor to Rosslyn Elder's private quarters.

The first floor of the gambling house had been fairly crowded, but apparently Rosslyn had closed the top floor after her assailant had left her. The local physician had just left, and the colored girl was sitting at Rosslyn's bedside when Mulvane knocked lightly on the door.

The colored girl opened it for him, stared at him for a moment, and then said gloomily, "She ain't pretty no more, Mr. Mulvane."

Mulvane walked past her to the bed and stared down. Rosslyn had her face turned toward the wall, but he could see the lumps, cuts and bruises, the blood-swollen right eye.

Anger raging inside of him, he sat down on the edge of the bed. "You saw who did it," he said. "Tell me."

Rosslyn shook her head, still not looking at him.

"It was Baudine," Mulvane said. "Wasn't it?"

This time she didn't shake her head and he had his answer. He sat there for some time, helpless, knowing that only time would heal that battered and bruised face.

"The man who did it," he said softly, "was less than a man, and he'll pay."

He put a hand on Rosslyn Elder's shoulder gently and went out. Down below on the main floor he spoke to one of the floormen near the stairway. He was a big, chunky-shouldered fellow with a red neck and ring-scarred face, the face of an expugilist.

Mulvane said to him, "You watch her games

down here but you don't watch her. Is that it?"

The floorman scowled. "Hell," he said, "we never figured on anything like this. She's up in her rooms. We're down here. I guess that dog just walked in when nobody was lookin'."

"If anybody walks in again," Mulvane told him gently, "I'm coming back here to shoot you."

The floorman stared. "Don't ride a man too hard," he said. "You think we feel good about this?"

Mulvane walked past him to the bar where Joe Smith was waiting. Smith said, "Baudine?"

Mulvane nodded.

"He was in here tonight," the gunman told him. "It adds up. But you won't find him in this town, you know."

"I know," Mulvane nodded. "We're riding out."

"Where?" Joe Smith asked.

"Von Dreber's," Mulvane said. "Baudine will be there."

Joe Smith started to grin. "Right into the damned lion's den," he chuckled.

The gunman had ordered a bottle and he pushed the bottle and a glass toward Mulvane. He said when Mulvane had poured himself a drink, "To Varney Baudine's black soul. May it rot in hell."

They left Wickburg, taking the stage road north this time in the direction of Von Dreber's castle. Starlight flooded the white ribbon of a road which pushed north into the hills. They picked up the lights from the southbound stage shortly after leaving town, and as it passed the driver flicked his whip toward them in greeting,

Joe Smith said, "You figure you'll walk right in there an' shoot the hell out of them. They'll shoot back, you know."

Mulvane just nodded. He'd had his look at Rosslyn Elder's face this night and he'd made a vow that Varney Baudine would not see the morning. He intended to keep that vow one way or the other.

"We'll make our plans after we get there," he said.

An hour out of Wickburg they saw the lights of the castle on a high hill north and west of the road.

"One thing," Joe Smith said. "They won't be lookin' for you, Mulvane. That's for sure."

They turned into a wagon trace which led up toward the castle. Hanging from the cottonwood archway over the trace was a large metal escutcheon with the swastika brand emblazoned in the center.

They had to climb a low hill to reach the huge stone structure. From the size of the building, now that he could see it close up, Mulvane supposed that it would contain at least twenty or thirty rooms. It was square in appearance, built like a box with four squat towers on the corners, and a central, pinnacle-like tower climbing quite high above the mass of stone.

There was no beauty about the building, but Von Dreber had built it solidly, destined to last a thousand years. In a way it was like the man, massive, with no pretensions, a symbol of brute strength and power.

As they neared the castle Mulvane turned the claybank off the trace and swung around toward the rear to come up behind the log bunkhouse set some distance from the stone structure.

They dismounted in the shadow of a clump of cottonwoods along the creek at the base of the hill, and then they moved on foot, coming up behind the bunkhouse.

There were only a few horses in the nearby corral, and Joe Smith said in a low voice, "Could be most of the crew are out with the herd. Von Dreber might be figurin' we're still cuttin' stock out."

Carefully, they made their way to the door of the bunkhouse, which was slightly ajar. Drawing his gun, Mulvane stepped up to the door, nodded to Joe Smith, and then suddenly kicked the door in and stepped into the room, gun in hand.

The long bunkhouse with its double tiers of bunks on either side of the big fireplace was empty save for two men playing cards at the rough table near the fireplace. One of the men was big Jug Streiber of the straw-colored hair and the vacant blue eyes. The other man was smaller, a leather-faced man with outcropping ears and a long nose.

Streiber's hand reached for the gun in the holster dangling from the chair next to him. When he saw the gun in Mulvane's hand, though, he put his hand back on the table.

Moving up to the table Mulvane said in a low voice, "Where's Baudine?"

"Hell with you," Streiber told him, and Mulvane hit him across the face with the back of his hand sending him tumbling off the chair to the hard-packed dirt floor.

Jug Streiber came up cursing, face twisted in rage. He looked at Mulvane and then at Joe Smith standing near the door, gun in hand, and he made no move to get up.

Mulvane said to the smaller man in a toneless voice, "So where's Baudine?"

The little puncher swallowed, grimaced, and then said, "Up in the big house."

Mulvane lifted the guns from the two holsters on the chairs, dropped them at Joe Smith's feet and said, "I'll be back."

"Come alive," Joe Smith told him, the grin on his face. "I'll be damned lonely here, mister."

CHAPTER 9

It was fifty yards from the bunkhouse to the castle. Mulvane walked across the hard-packed earth toward the main entrance, passing several smaller outbuildings. A rounded stone portico extended out from the door, supported by stone pillars.

Mulvane stepped in under the portico seeing in the dim light that the huge, oaken door had a knocker on it. Stepping up to the door he raised the knocker and rapped hard several times.

The door opened and the short, stocky, bulbous-nosed Hans Krauss stuck his head out.

"*Vas?*" Krauss asked.

Mulvane drew his gun and jammed it into the German's belly, making him gasp. Then spinning him around by the shoulder he marched him on ahead down a short corridor which opened on to what must have been the main waiting room or lounge room. An enormous fireplace, large enough for a man to walk around inside, took up one side of the room.

Mulvane had a glimpse of several pieces of statuary, one undoubtedly a bust of the German political leader, Bismarck. A huge oak table stood in the center of the room, and there were heavy oak chairs scattered along the wall. A big settee stood in front of the fireplace.

Varney Baudine had been sitting on the settee apparently waiting for Von Dreber to make his appearance. He'd had his back toward Mulvane but he turned and looked now, hearing the steps on the stone floor.

With his free hand Mulvane pushed Hans Krauss to one side as Baudine, his nose still plastered with the dirty tape came to his feet. Baudine wore the Colt gun on his hip as he backed a few steps away from the settee, his opaque eyes narrowed, staring at Mulvane.

Mulvane said softly, "Come for you, Baudine."

Varney Baudine licked his lips with the tip of his tongue. His eyes flicked to the right and to the left.

"You got your damned nerve coming in here, mister," he said.

Mulvane said, "You were at the El Dorado this evening, Baudine. You know why I'm here."

Baudine's eyes moved to the gun in Mulvane's hand, and then to Hans Krauss staring at them from the wall. Then he glanced toward the stairway which led to the upper floor sleeping rooms. His eyes moved all the time like little mice on the run.

"You worked on Miss Elder with your fists while you were at the El Dorado," Mulvane went on, no emotion in his voice.

"That right?" Baudine murmured. His eyes were still moving, and Mulvane could almost read his mind. Varney Baudine was weighing his chances, looking desperately for the little edge he liked to have when drawing his gun, but it wasn't here this evening, and he wasn't too happy about it. His right hand taut at his side, he waited, staring at the gun in Mulvane's hand again. His body settled now in a half crouch and a kind of sigh escaped him. It was as if he'd now made up his mind and was glad that the moment of indecision had gone and he knew what he had to do.

His boots flat on the floor, spread, well-balanced, he waited. Mulvane said softly but distinctly, "You're dead, Baudine. Draw your gun."

Then he slipped his own back into the holster and he waited.

Baudine put out his left hand as if to adjust a cushion on the settee nearby and then very suddenly, very speedily, his right hard moved. The gun was out of the holster when Mulvane's first bullet struck him in the chest, blasting him back toward the stone wall to the left of the fireplace.

Baudine's gun boomed as he smashed back into the wall. His hat fell from his head as he spun, his eyes blinking rapidly, trying to focus on Mulvane across the room.

His gun was coming up again, wavering, searching out for his opponent when Mulvane sent another bullet at him, this time catching him between the eyes. He went down like a stone, dead before he hit the floor, the gun bouncing from his hand, rattling across the stone floor. He lay in a crumpled heap against the wall, no more a man, looking like a collapsed scarecrow.

The gun still smoking in his hand, Mulvane looked toward the wide staircase which led to the upper floor, and he was surprised to see the Countess Hilda Hannau standing halfway down, one white hand touching the railing. She was a radiant figure in pure white, low-cut dress revealing her full bosom, a diamond necklace gleaming at her throat.

She had undoubtedly been coming down the stairs as Baudine had drawn his gun, and she'd seen the fight. She'd seen Baudine fall down and die, and there was a strange look on her beautiful face. It was not fear; it was not shock. She was not smiling, but Mulvane could clearly see the pleasure in her beautiful blue eyes!

Von Dreber came down the stairs behind her, wearing a strange blue and gold half-jacket with a fur collar. The jacket came down below the hips and was pulled in with a gold sash.

Pausing just below the step where the Countess Hannau was standing, Von Dreber stared down at Mulvane and then at the sprawled figure of Baudine over near the fireplace wall.

At that moment with the gun still in his hand Mulvane saw Trasker Flynn come in through the door which opened on the huge oaken dining room and kitchen beyond. He'd apparently been in the kitchen having a late meal because his jaws were still working on food as he stepped into the room.

Shaking with rage, Von Dreber pointed one quivering finger at Mulvane and then he roared, "Kill him!"

Mulvane looked at Trasker Flynn across the room. Flynn's jaws had stopped working and he looked up at Von Dreber, a small smile on his face. He said softly, "Reckon he's got the jump on me again, Mr. Von Dreber."

Carefully, Mulvane backed toward the door, leaving Von Dreber speechless on the stairway. Passing out through the huge door he raced back to the bunkhouse where Joe Smith was still holding his gun on the two Von Dreber riders.

Smith said, "All right?"

"All right," Mulvane nodded. He picked up the two guns at Smith's feet, tossing them out into the darkness, and then both men left the bunkhouse, moving at a run to the creek where they'd left their horses.

"He dead?" Joe Smith asked as they ran.

"Dead," Mulvane told him.

"You run into Trasker Flynn?"

"I had the drop on him," Mulvane said soberly, and he wondered what would have happened if he hadn't.

• • •

In the morning Charlie O'Leary said as they were sipping coffee near the fire, "You don't figure Von Dreber will let you get away with this, do you?"

"We'll see," Mulvane said easily.

Charlie nodded soberly and then rolled a cigarette. He said, "Figure I'd better head up to Moose Creek and pick up that stock Sam Holloway's been holdin' for me. Sam's itchin' to pull out an' I'm gittin' this stuff fer the low dollar. Lost damn near half my herd to Von Dreber an' I only got back part of it."

Mulvane sipped a cup of coffee. "How far is Moose River?" he asked.

"Ten miles south an' west," Charlie told him. "One day's drive fer two men. Meigs could look after things here."

Mulvane put the tin cup down. "Reckon I'll ride with you," he said. "Leave now. Start them moving in the morning."

Charlie scratched his chin. "Wouldn't hurt for you to get the hell out o' this country fer a day or two, Mulvane."

Mulvane smiled. "I figure on pushing Von Dreber all the way," he pointed out. "If we bring in more stock we're showing him that we're here to stay."

They saddled up and were preparing to leave when Ben Meigs called from the shack, "Rider comin' up."

Mulvane watched Trasker Flynn on his small blue roan lope down the side of a low hill and then cross a flat to the creek. Charlie O'Leary said worriedly, "You figure Von Dreber sent him to square things up with you?"

Mulvane shook his head. "Even Flynn wouldn't ride into a camp this big," he said.

Flynn rode up, his hat on the back of his head, a smile on his face.

Mulvane said to him, "Coffee?"

"Don't mind if I do," Trasker Flynn nodded, and he stepped down from the saddle.

Mulvane said as he poured a cup of hot coffee from the pot on the fire, "In the wrong camp, Trasker."

The little gunman just shrugged and looked over at the group of men seated on the ground under a big cottonwood tree. He nodded to Bill Smith whom he evidently had known before.

"Man like you must have a reason for coming here," Mulvane said as Flynn sipped the coffee.

Flynn looked at Charlie O'Leary across the fire and said nothing. Charlie put his hands in his back pockets and walked off, whistling to himself. Flynn said evenly, "Figured you'd like to know, Mulvane. Von Dreber has given orders and a special bonus to three of his dogs to gun you down—any damn way they like."

Mulvane tossed a twig into the fire. "Whose side you on, Trasker?" he asked softly.

"Not the side of bushwhackers," Flynn growled. "These three wouldn't stand up against you. They'll be going for your back."

"Know them?" Mulvane asked.

"Big fellow with the yellow hair is one," Flynn said. "Goes by the name of Streiber. Two others like him. Figure Von Dreber is paying them real high for this job. That's the only job they have now. They'll be watching you day and night."

"Why didn't Von Dreber send you?" Mulvane asked him curiously.

"He knew damned well I wouldn't go," Flynn said. "That's not my kind of job."

"Still riding for him?"

Flynn looked up and down the creek, his brown eyes moving over the groups of stock grazing on the north slope above the creek. He said, "Reckon I signed up to drive some damned rustlers out of this country. I took a month's wages in advance and I dropped the money in a card game. Reckon I still owe damn near a month to Von Dreber."

Mulvane nodded. He watched Trasker Flynn sipping his coffee, and then he said, "Streiber didn't tell you he'd be gunning for me, and Von Dreber didn't, either. It was somebody else."

Flynn smiled at him across the rim of the coffee cup. "You figure who," he said easily, and Mulvane had no difficulty getting the answer.

"Way I look at it," Flynn observed, "that woman came a long way to learn that the man she was going to marry wasn't the man she wants to marry now."

Mulvane said nothing to this, and then Flynn moved over to his horse and stepped into the saddle.

"I'm obliged," Mulvane said.

"Watch your back," Flynn warned him and he rode off.

Mulvane considered for a few moments whether he ought to ride into Wickburg to see Rosslyn Elder before leaving for Moose Creek but decided against it. In her condition Rosslyn would want no company, especially male company. The woman was proud of her looks.

At eleven o'clock in the morning he rode off with Charlie O'Leary headed south and west in the direction of Moose Creek where the rancher Holloway was grazing his stock.

The day was hot again, a clear, windless, cloudless day with the heat devils dancing in the distance. They crossed a series of low hills, followed a dry creek bed for a mile or so, and then climbed up through a narrow pass choked with low, dwarf pines.

After they'd threaded their way through the pass Mulvane pulled up the claybank and stared back down the trail.

Charlie O'Leary said thoughtfully, "Third time you did that, Mulvane. You figure somebody's doggin' us?"

Mulvane shook his head. An hour before he'd seen a tiny column of dust a long distance behind them which could or could not mean other riders. Moving through this pass he'd again had the feeling that someone was coming along behind them.

He said suddenly, "Ride on, Charlie. I'll double back."

Charlie frowned, but he pushed his horse through the pines. Mulvane circled up on higher ground, gradually swinging back toward the dim trail through the pass. He rode back a mile or two before reaching the trail again, and then seeing only two sets of hoofbeats in the dirt he shook his head in disgust and rode on again to catch up with O'Leary. He was quite convinced in his mind now that his imagination had been playing tricks with him. Either that, or the men following him were uncannily good at keeping their distance and still not letting their quarry move too far ahead of them.

When he caught up with Charlie O'Leary the little rancher said, "Shyin' at shadows, Mulvane?"

Mulvane just shook his head as they rode on again. By mid-afternoon they reached Moose Creek, and an hour later they came upon Sam Holloway and the single rider with him, camped along the south bank of the creek, with his small herd of stock grazing on the nearby hills.

Holloway, a tall, gaunt man with a hatchet jaw, said sourly, "You took your damned time, O'Leary. Just gettin' ready to move on with this stock."

"You run too fast, Sam," O'Leary grinned. "You'll move faster without these beeves, though, won't you? So it was worth waitin'."

The remainder of the afternoon, while the three men rounded up the stock and bunched them along the creek, Mulvane rode back down the trail a second time, and it was dusk when he returned, having seen nothing. If Streiber and his two cutthroats actually were dogging them all the way down here, it was evident that they were not going to make any kind of stand-up fight.

Because Sam Holloway was anxious to move on, Charlie O'Leary paid him for the stock late that afternoon, received his bill of sale, and then they watched as Holloway and his rider headed down along the Moose and out of the country.

Charlie said, "Reckon that's the kind Von Dreber likes—the kind that runs."

In the light of the campfire they'd kicked together Charlie got his coffee pot out of the saddlebag and was grinding his coffee when the rifle cracked from the grade behind them. The bullet grazed Mulvane's ribs, smashing the handle off the coffee pot, sending it spinning into the dirt.

Both men dived out of the light of the fire,

Mulvane snatching his Winchester rifle out of the holster on the ground. In the darkness now he circled, trying to pin-point the spot from which the shot had come, but his back had been turned to the rifleman and he hadn't seen the flash of the gun. There had been one shot and no more.

He paused once to listen carefully, thinking that he might hear the sound of a horse moving away, but there were no sounds. He went up the grade, keeping down low, the rifle in readiness, but when he'd made a half-circle and still hadn't flushed his man, he stood up, hearing Charlie coming up the grade on the opposite side.

He called softly, "All right, Charlie."

"Flush him?" Charlie asked.

"Gone," Mulvane growled.

Charlie came up in the dim starlight. "Reckon you were right, Mulvane," he said grimly. "Somebody's been on our tail ever since we left the camp. Figure you know them?"

"Jug Streiber's one," Mulvane said, and he was thinking that the other two would be a lot smarter than Streiber to get up close to his campfire, send a bullet at his back, and then move away without being seen.

"They got away tonight," Charlie O'Leary said grimly, "an' I reckon that means they'll be watchin' fer us on the way back tomorrow."

Mulvane started to walk back toward the fire.

He said over his shoulder, an edge to his voice, "We'll be watching for them, too."

"That big ape Streiber's been itching fer a belly full o' lead fer a long time," Charlie O'Leary observed. "Sooner or later he'll be gettin' it."

That night Mulvane slept with his gun inches away from his face even though he was quite sure Streiber and the killers with him would not return again this evening. They were dealing now with snakes, and it was difficult ascertaining exactly what a snake would do at any given time.

CHAPTER 10

They were up before dawn, Charlie O'Leary cooking a hasty breakfast, and they started the small herd toward the north just as the sun was coming up. They pushed the stock toward the pass through which they had come the previous day.

Charlie said once as he passed Mulvane, "They'll be waitin'."

Mulvane nodded. He knew something that O'Leary didn't know. These hired killers were not after stock; they wanted the hide of Mulvane!

It was slow work pushing the stock up into the pass. Charlie pointed them north and Mulvane brought up the drag, his bandanna drawn up over his mouth and nose to keep out the dust, his gray eyes searching the pines every moment as he rode, ready to snatch the Winchester from the saddle holster at a moment's notice.

It was the kind of warfare he hated. Standing up to a man was one thing. Knowing that a bullet might come from ambush at any moment was another, and he had his opinion of men who would shoot from the brush and then run. One thing he knew; if they opened up on him he was going after them, and he wasn't going to stop until one or more were dead.

Several times as they moved through the pass Charlie looked back in Mulvane's direction as he pushed his leaders on. Moving higher and higher into the pass, Mulvane realized that it would be here that the bushwhackers would make their attempt, if any place. There were wooded hills on either side of them now and dozens of men could hide on those slopes, rifles in readiness, and still not be seen.

Charlie held up the stock and rode back to meet Mulvane. He said when he came up, "Only takes one of us to push this bunch through the pass. We'll be stayin' on the low ground. Might be smart if you circled up along one o' these ridges."

"Makes sense," Mulvane agreed.

As Charlie worked his rope and got the stock moving again Mulvane swung off toward the right, climbing up among the pines. If the bushwhackers were concealed in the pass they would very shortly discover that Charlie was coming through alone. They would be watching for their prey but now they would not be positive where he was, and this evened up the odds somewhat.

Mulvane rode slowly, the Winchester out of the holster, letting the claybank pick its own way along the side of the hill. Down below at the bottom of the pass he could hear Charlie O'Leary faintly as he pushed the stock on over the trace, and he could see the cloud of dust marking their passage.

When they were nearly halfway through the pass he dismounted, leading the claybank behind as he pushed forward on foot, both man and animal making very little sound on the thick bed of pine needles.

Up here he could see very little, but he could still hear Charlie O'Leary down below. If the ambushers were concealed on this side of the pass, they would have to be somewhat lower if they wanted to get a clear shot at a man moving along the trace.

Still leading the claybank, Mulvane started down the grade, moving cautiously now, stopping occasionally to listen. He hadn't gone more than two hundred yards when he spotted the sorrel horse tied among the pines.

Pulling up abruptly he moved the claybank out of sight, tying the animal to the branch of a tree, and then with the Winchester in his hand, he moved forward silently, keeping the pines between himself and the sorrel. Now he spotted a second and a third horse close by, a chestnut gelding and a steel gray. He still didn't see the three bushwhackers, but he knew now that they were close by, farther down the slope beyond the spot where they'd left their mounts.

Carefully, Mulvane worked his way around the horses, still going downgrade. Twenty-five yards below the spot where the horses had been tied he slid down into a small pothole in the side of the hill. The hole was about a half-dozen yards across and quite steep.

Crouching, he crossed the pothole and then crawled up to the rim on the opposite side, positive that the ambushers were very close by now. He could hear the stock coming up the pass almost adjacent to the spot where he was concealed, and he could clearly hear Charlie O'Leary's quick shouts,

Lifting his head cautiously, Mulvane looked down the slope, which was dotted with pines. They were considerably thinner here, though, and he could see all the way down to the bottom of the pass to the faint trace which ran through it.

Two men crouched behind a big outcropping of rock on the side of the hill, their backs toward him as they lay sprawled on the ground, rifles pushed down toward the pass. The man on the right was a big fellow with heavy shoulders and a shock of light, yellowish hair. Mulvane had no difficulty in recognizing Jug Streiber.

The second man had his hat off as he lay on the ground beside Streiber and his head was semibald. Mulvane watched them from a distance of less than a hundred feet, a frown coming to his face. He lay there on the wall of the pothole, remembering that there had been three horses, and Flynn had informed him that three men had been set aside for the task of killing him. There were only two men below.

It may have been this fact which accounted for his next move, or it may have been the sixth sense which told him that danger was close by. In all probability, though, it was more his uncanny sense of hearing which saved his life.

He half-imagined that he heard a light step behind him, not a crunching bootstep, but more like an Indian moccasin, coming down on the padding of pine needles, making almost no sound.

Instinctively, Mulvane rolled to his right just as a gun exploded. The ambusher who'd come up behind him had been less than a dozen yards away when he fired. He was a tall, lean fellow with blue-black hair, black eyes, and his skin was dark brown. He could have been an Indian or a breed. His nose was the nose of an Indian, fierce, hooked, with a thin slit of a mouth beneath it.

The bushwhacker was in white man's clothing—faded blue Levi's, a leather jacket decorated with silver spangles. In place of boots, though, he wore high Indian moccasins. With that first quick glimpse of the man Mulvane was convinced that he was the one who'd crawled down close to their fire the previous evening to fire that single shot and then disappear without any difficulty.

Swinging the Winchester, Mulvane got off one quick snapshot, knowing it was too hurried, but it was meant only to disconcert the breed, who would be trying to get off his second shot.

He rolled again even as he fired the Winchester, and the bullet from the breed's gun knocked a sliver of rock from the rim of the pothole. The bushwhacker turned then and ran abruptly up the slope, darting in and out among the trees, making it impossible for Mulvane to get off a second shot at him.

Crossing the pothole Mulvane scrambled out, took one look down the grade toward Jug Streiber, noticing that both men had dived for cover when the fusilade had begun above them. He took out after the running breed who was still going uphill like a hunted deer headed for the safety of higher ground.

He'd angled away from the three horses, and this move surprised Mulvane as he followed the man. The breed was very agile moving on light moccasins, and Mulvane was considering whether it would be wiser to head back for the claybank and then take up the chase, but he realized that even a horse would not catch a fast-moving Indian on terrain like this, and by the time he returned with the claybank the breed would definitely have disappeared.

He decided to continue the chase on foot, hoping to get within range of his man before he reached the summit of the slope. They had gone about two hundred yards up the grade, Mulvane moving as fast as he could with the clumsy boots when suddenly the breed disappeared.

Mulvane stared unbelievingly as he pulled up behind a low pine. One moment he'd caught a glimpse of the man running, and the next moment he was gone.

Warily, Mulvane circled the spot where he'd seen the runner. Dropping down on his stomach then he lay still and waited, convinced that the bushwhacker was very close by. He remembered then how suddenly he'd come upon the pothole down below, and it was very possible that another of these unusual formations lay farther up the grade and the breed had dropped into one of them and was now waiting, gun drawn.

Mulvane lay on his stomach on the pine needles, concealed from above by the thick branches of the long-needled pine behind which he'd fallen. He lay perfectly still, his breath coming and going easily. He lay still for several minutes until he'd completely recovered from his hard run up the hill, and then casually he rolled over on his back and lay on the pine needles, his hat to one side, looking up at the sky.

It was going to be a duel of patience now, the patience of the Indian against the patience of the white man, and sooner or later one of them would have to make a move. Mulvane was convinced it would not be he!

As he lay on his back he could hear horses moving off on the hill and he surmised that Streiber and his partner were moving out, leaving the breed behind. Undoubtedly, Charlie O'Leary was now working his way carefully up the grade, also, and Streiber did not like to be caught between two fires. Coldly, therefore, he was riding away, and to hell with the breed who lay in his pothole.

Mulvane lay still on the pine needles, partly concealed by the overhanging boughs. He listened carefully but he could no longer hear the horses, and his lip curled in contempt as he thought of Strieber pulling out of this scrap now that their man was ready and waiting for them.

A bluejay flew into one of the branches overhead, spotted him on the ground, chattered once, and then flew away. Rolling over on his stomach, the Winchester pushed ahead of him, Mulvane watched the spot where he supposed the pothole would be. He was convinced now that the breed lay there as silent as a snake, waiting for his man to reveal himself.

He had been lying on the pine needles for almost a quarter of an hour now, and it was impossible to foresee how much longer he would have had to wait had not Charlie O'Leary come riding up the hill.

Mulvane heard the horse first, and then a short while later O'Leary calling sharply, "Mulvane—Mulvane?"

Frowning, Mulvane lifted his sixgun and shot into the air, and then rolled a half dozen yards away as a rifle bullet felt for him from the pothole up the grade.

The warning shot had stopped Charlie O'Leary, though, and Mulvane heard him no more. He lay on his stomach staring toward the spot where a small cloud of rifle smoke lifted up into the air. By his warning shot to O'Leary he had at least ascertained the location of the pothole.

He started to move now, crawling flat on his stomach, knowing that Charlie would stay back. He had this advantage over the breed as he worked his way toward the right. The bushwhacker had to look downhill to see him, which meant that he would have to raise his body slightly above the rim of the hole. If he raised it a little too high he was going to be dead.

Still watching the spot from which the shot had come Mulvane continued his half-circle, trying always to keep a tree in between himself and the hole as he moved.

The breed kept out of sight, undoubtedly knowing the advantage Mulvane had now, and not willing to let him benefit by it. There were no sounds except the bawling of the stock down in the pass.

When he was still some twenty-five yards from the pothole, almost parallel with it now on the hill, Mulvane stopped and again rolled over on his back. He was in a small indentation, the hole barely concealing him as he lay flat.

With the Winchester at his side he reached into his shirt pocket for his sack of tobacco. Leisurely, lying on his back, he rolled a cigarette, and still flat on his back, put it in his mouth, touching a match to it. He took several puffs on the cigarette to get it going, and then, reaching up, he jammed the lighted, smoking cigarette into a twig on a line with his face.

Easily, then, he crawled another half-dozen yards away, leaving the smoking cigarette. It was only a matter of time now before the sharp-eyed breed discovered the cigarette smoke and made his play.

Mulvane carefully cocked the hammer of the Winchester, lying on his stomach with the muzzle of the gun pointed toward the pothole. He waited, his body concealed behind some pine seedlings. From where he lay he could see the tiny curl of smoke lifting from the burning cigarette.

He imagined that the cigarette was nearly burned through when the breed took action. The barrel of a rifle was suddenly thrust over the rim of the pothole, and then the breed's face came into view as he quickly took aim and fired at the cigarette, the roar of the gun filling the pass.

At the same instant Mulvane lined the Winchester on his target and squeezed on the trigger. The pothole was considerably smaller than he'd imagined it to be because the breed suddenly stood up, the upper half of his body revealed from the waist up, and then he fell backward.

Lifting the sixgun from the holster, carrying the Winchester in his free hand, Mulvane moved forward. He had the gun in readiness but it was unnecessary, because when he came to the pothole he saw the breed lying flat on his back with a bullet hole between the eyes, as dead as he would ever be. His rifle lay beside him where it had fallen.

Holstering the sixgun Mulvane called loudly, "All right, Charlie."

Charlie O'Leary came up the hill carrying his rifle. He looked down at the dead breed and he said, "There were three of them."

"Streiber and his partner pulled out," Mulvane said. "This one holed up." He paused and he said, "Know him Charlie?"

"Goes by the name of Blassingame," Charlie said. "Loose rider Von Dreber picked up. Part Crow I reckon, but it don't matter now any more. Must o' been pretty good at trackin' a man down."

"Find his horse down below," Mulvane said. "We'll pack him in to town."

Charlie went down the grade, a few minutes later coming back with the sorrel horse. They tied the breed's body to the saddle and then moved down the grade again, Mulvane picking up the claybank on the way.

With Mulvane coming on behind with the dead man, Charlie O'Leary moved on ahead to pick up the stock they'd left in the pass, and it was late afternoon when they reached the camp on the creek.

Charlie moved the new stock in with the combined herds of the small ranchers, and then joined Mulvane as they approached the line camp.

Joe Smith said as they came up, "Reckon you boys did a little more than push cows today. Who's your friend?"

"Bushwhacker," Charlie scowled. "Von Dreber's boy."

Joe Smith looked at the body of the breed and he said, "Reckon this one didn't make it, Mulvane."

Charlie O'Leary said to Mulvane, "Takin' him in to town?"

"I'll take him in," Mulvane said, "alone."

Charlie frowned. "You're askin' for trouble," he observed.

Mulvane smiled faintly. He was thinking now of Rosslyn Elder being beaten up, of three men trying to bushwhack him back in the pass. The pressure was more than he liked, and it was time that somebody else started to feel it.

He had a cup of coffee at the fire, Charlie O'Leary still watching him glumly.

"Whole damned Von Dreber crowd is out to

gun you," Charlie said. "You want to go right into town alone?"

"Men have tried to gun me before," Mulvane observed.

He rode off a few minutes later, taking the dead bushwhacker with him, and he'd nearly reached the stage road when he saw two riders coming on behind him. He pulled up and waited, recognizing Joe and Bill Smith.

The two gunmen came on slowly, both smoking cigarettes, and when they drew up to him he said shortly, "Where in hell you boys figure you're going?"

"Wickburg," Joe Smith grinned. "Ain't no law against a man ridin' into town, is there?"

Bill Smith said, "O'Leary figured he'd give us the night off. That's fair enough, ain't it?"

"If somebody runs O'Leary's stock off tonight," Mulvane scowled, "that'll be fair, too."

"Only cows," Joe Smith laughed. "Man can buy more cows."

CHAPTER 11

The three of them rode on together, and it was dusk when they reached the town, Mulvane moving on to the sheriff's office with the dead man, and the two Smith boys dismounting across the way.

A small crowd quickly gathered around the dead man as Mulvane went up to the sheriff's office where a light was burning in the window. Walking into the room he found the rancher Ed Grimes of Slash G, chair tilted against the wall, talking with McAdams. Grimes stared at Mulvane, dislike in his eyes.

McAdams had been in the act of lighting up a cigar, but he took the cigar out of his mouth now and stared at Mulvane grimly.

"What in hell do you want?" the lawman scowled.

"Dead man outside," Mulvane told him. "Man by the name of Blassingame. Tried to bushwhack me up near Moose Creek."

McAdams looked at Ed Grimes and Grimes shook his head.

"Not my rider," Grimes said.

"Rides for Von Dreber," Mulvane told them.

"What in hell do you want me to do?" McAdams snapped. "Moose Creek is out of my territory."

"Figured you'd like to know," Mulvane said. "Blassingame comes from this territory. You can tell his boss the next time he sends one of his dogs after me I'm going after him."

"Tell him yourself," McAdams said tersely, and then he got up from the chair and walked over to the door to look out at the dead breed.

Ed Grimes said from the chair, "You walk pretty big in this country, mister. I've seen them walk big before but they end up like that rider out front."

Mulvane was convinced in his own mind that Grimes knew nothing about Blassingame being sent to bushwhack him. Grimes was a tough, blunt-nosed, avaricious rancher like so many other big men on the range, willing and ready to ride roughshod over the small men. But he was above bushwhacking.

Mulvane said to him, "You're riding with a pretty low crowd, Grimes, and some day you'll find out about it."

He went outside then, pushing past McAdams at the door. As he went down on the walk he saw a buckboard coming along the street and immediately recognized the square-shouldered man at the reins. Hilda Hannau, in range clothes now—black, flat-crowned hat, flannel shirt and Levi's—sat beside Von Dreber on the seat.

Seeing the small knot of men out in front of the sheriff's office, Von Dreber pulled up the big grays he was driving. Mulvane saw him stare at the dead man draped across the saddle. From his position, Von Dreber couldn't see the face of the dead rider, but a man nearby called softly, "One o' your boys, Mr. Von Dreber. Ira Blassingame."

The Countess Hannau had spotted Mulvane on the walk, and she was looking past Von Dreber straight at him as he stood there. Mulvane stepped down off the walk, circled the horse with the dead man tied to the saddle, and stood a few feet from Von Dreber's buckboard. He said flatly, anger in his voice, "Your rider tried to bushwhack me, Von Dreber. I had to kill him."

Von Dreber stared down at him, his rocklike face as hard as iron.

"What is it you want?" he snapped.

"Reckon you sent this dog," Mulvane told him, "and before you ride out of town tonight I'm expecting satisfaction."

The Prussian army officer did not appear as if he were quite sure what Mulvane wanted. "Satisfaction?" he repeated.

"You've been sending other men to do your dirty work," Mulvane said evenly. "Now try to do some of it yourself. I'll be waiting for you in the El Dorado."

He touched his hat to the Countess Hannau, seeing her beautiful face in the dim light, and then he turned and moved on, heading toward the

El Dorado. As he walked he heard the low hum from the crowd.

At the El Dorado he went directly upstairs to Rosslyn Elder's rooms, knocked on the door, and was admitted. He found Rosslyn sitting up in bed having her supper. Her face was still puffed, but she was in considerably better spirits now.

"You killed Baudine," she said. "I suppose I should be flattered."

"Baudine had it coming," Mulvane said, "sooner or later." He sat down in the chair beside her and watched as she poured a cup of coffee for him, watching him as he picked up the cup.

"How is it going out at Charlie's place?" she asked.

Mulvane told her briefly of their ride down to Moose Creek and of the attempted ambush on the way back.

"Got the new stock up on the range," he finished, "and Charlie figures on staying."

"You're still fighting them," she said. "I'm glad."

"Tonight I might fight the big one, himself," Mulvane smiled at her over the coffee cup.

Rosslyn stared. "Von Dreber?" she asked.

"Figures that way," Mulvane nodded. "He won't come with a gun because he knows that I can kill him, but he'll come."

"He'll never stop trying to kill you," Rosslyn frowned.

"Or he's killed himself," Mulvane said. He finished the coffee and stood up. "How long before you'll be downstairs?" he asked.

Rosslyn shook her head. "I don't want to show myself like this," she said. "Soon."

Mulvane went downstairs and saw Joe and Bill Smith waiting for him at the bar.

"Takin' Von Dreber tonight?" Joe Smith asked.

"He's been invited," Mulvane nodded.

"Tell me he never carries a gun," Joe Smith observed. "A Dutchman like that wouldn't know how to use it, anyway."

"We'll see," Mulvane said. He ordered drinks for the two riders and when they'd downed the drinks he said, "This is my fight. Stay out of it."

"As long as there's only one of them," Joe Smith grinned, "an' one o' you. Seems to me this Von Dreber don't like even odds, though."

A little old man with a seamed face hurried in through the bat-wing doors, coming up to Mulvane. He said in a low voice, "Von Dreber's still down at the hotel. They're dinin' out tonight."

Mulvane nodded. "Watch them for me, Grandpa," he said, and the old man ran out, very eager, very happy.

Crossing to the restaurant on the opposite side of the street, Mulvane had his supper, eating light tonight, the conviction coming to him that he'd have to be in pretty good physical shape if Von Dreber stepped into the El Dorado.

The stove-in puncher who waited on him as he sat at the counter said, "Hear you're takin' on the Dutchman tonight, Mr. Mulvane."

Mulvane went on eating, shrugging his shoulders slightly.

"Be a damned good thing for this town," the waiter scowled, "if somebody knocks that sausage-eater off his high horse."

"Might be the other way around," Mulvane smiled. "Don't talk too fast, my friend."

He ate leisurely, lightly, a small steak and coffee, and then he smoked a cigar all the way through before getting up from his chair and moving out toward the street. As he stood in the doorway he saw the crowd around the El Dorado as word had spread through Wickburg that he had called Von Dreber out.

He saw Neil McAdams staring up the street from out in front of the sheriff's office. The two Smiths were lounging on one corner of the El Dorado porch, just waiting.

The weazened old man who had apparently elected himself as Mulvane's aide in the coming conflict hurried up the street and said to Mulvane, "They're still eatin'. The damned Dutchman eats like a pig."

"I'm obliged," Mulvane said.

The old man scooted off again to keep an eye on Von Dreber. Crossing the road, Mulvane pushed through the crowd and into the El Dorado again. The big floorman whom he'd asked to keep an eye on Rosslyn said to him, "You got this town stirred up, mister. You figure the Dutchman will come?"

"What are the odds?" Mulvane asked him.

"With guns it's a hundred to one for you," the floorman grinned. "Only he won't come with a gun. With his fists he'll be pretty rough. He has that look about him, and the Dutchmen never give up, you know."

Mulvane nodded.

"I figure he'll come," the floorman said, "but not with a gun."

Mulvane found a card game in a corner and sat down to play a few hands. As he was taking his seat the old man came to his elbow and whispered, "That feller Flynn just rode in. Figured you'd like to know, Mr. Mulvane."

Mulvane nodded. He played two hands and then he saw Trasker Flynn coming through the door. Flynn's brown eyes searched the room until they came to rest on him.

Mulvane pulled out of the game, moving up to the bar where Flynn was ordering a drink. He said, "Von Dreber send you, Trasker?"

Flynn shook his head. "Not me," he said. "I'm out of it."

Mulvane nodded.

Flynn said to him, "You'd better be damned

careful, Mulvane. That man's a bear. He could kill you with his hands."

"He could," Mulvane admitted.

He went back to his card game and sat down. He'd played three hands before the old man hurried into the saloon and whispered, the excitement making his voice shake, "He's comin'!"

Mulvane handed the old man a silver dollar and then said to the men with him at the card table, "I'm out."

He could hear the noise outside, the rising hum of excitement. Von Dreber came in through the doors, his cold blue eyes sweeping the room until they came to rest on Mulvane. He wasn't wearing a gun. He stood as stiff and as straight as a ramrod just inside the bat-wing doors, big shoulders tense. He was somewhat taller, and considerably heavier than Mulvane, flat in the waist, with powerful shoulders and arms.

Trasker Flynn, who had been standing at the bar, moved now to a far wall and put a shoulder against the wall to watch. The two Smiths stared at Von Dreber, and Mulvane saw Joe Smith shake his head glumly.

Pushing back his chair, Mulvane got up and walked between the tables toward the door. Von Dreber watched him come, bleak blue eyes narrowed.

"See you got here," Mulvane said.

"I'm here," Von Dreber snapped.

"You don't wear a gun," Mulvane observed, and Von Dreber stared at him, saying nothing.

Behind Von Dreber the doorway was jammed with faces, with people staring in through the windows which opened on the porch. All the games had stopped in the room. The four bartenders stood behind the long bar watching.

Mulvane unbuckled his gunbelt and turned and walked back to the bar, placing it on the wood. Then he came back to where Von Dreber was waiting and said, "We can take it outside."

He walked past the big Prussian then, pushing through the crowd at the doors. He went down the steps and out into the road which was fairly well lighted from the nearby buildings.

As he turned to face Von Dreber coming down the steps behind him he saw the Countess Hannau standing on the walk at the edge of the crowd watching, and he smiled a little. Knowing her as he did he'd been sure she would not want to miss a spectacle such as this.

There was surprisingly little noise. The crowd quickly formed an almost silent circle. There was no betting going around, which also surprised Mulvane.

Von Dreber had been wearing a heavy tweed jacket. He took it off now, draping it across the nearby tie rack, placing his flat-crowned hat on top of the coat. Then he walked out to where Mulvane was waiting for him, cool and poised, balanced lightly on the balls of his boots.

"Ready?" Mulvane asked him.

"*Yah*," Von Dreber said, and Mulvane stepped in fast, swinging hard for Von Dreber's stomach.

The fist got through, but his hand seemed to literally bounce off the powerful Prussian's midsection, almost as if he'd struck a piece of unyielding rubber. He knew, then, that he was in for the fight of his life. He'd hoped that Von Dreber would be soft around the middle from easy living, but this was not so.

Von Dreber was not a man who fought with his fists. He wanted it close up where he could get his hands on his man and use that brute strength and extra weight to break him.

Mulvane moved away from him, hearing the crowd begin to hum. When Von Dreber suddenly lunged in at him he punched with both hands to the Prussian's face, drawing blood on the left cheek and the right corner of his mouth. The blows seemed to have no more effect upon Von Dreber than mosquito bites. He came in stolidly, big hands extended, face like granite.

Mulvane hit him several more times, cutting him over the right eye this time so that the blood started to cascade over the eye, blinding him on the right side, but Von Dreber still came in, reaching, always reaching.

Wisely, Mulvane circled to his left keeping on Von Dreber's blind side, lashing with his fists and then moving back again. Once, as he tried to get out of the way, Von Dreber's heel caught him and he went down heavily.

As he hit the ground Von Dreber dived for him, reaching for his neck, but Mulvane rolled like a cat, coming up on his knees and then to his feet.

Von Dreber got up more slowly, and then did a curious thing. He dusted himself off carefully, and this was truly strange. With his face a bloody mask he still seemed quite concerned about dust on his clothing!

Still there was no noise from the crowd watching. This was no ordinary street brawl, Mulvane knew, and the crowd seemed to sense it, too. This was a fight to the death. Von Dreber had every intention of killing his man. It was written on his face, in his cold eyes, in the deliberate way he stalked his man, big hands extended.

The fight followed the same pattern for fully five minutes, Mulvane circling, keeping his distance, darting in and darting out, lashing with quick fists, cutting Von Dreber horribly, occasionally slamming hard fists into the heavier man's stomach. But Von Dreber seemed as strong as ever. It was not courage; it was something beyond courage; it was the strange, indomitable will of a man who could never even conceive of defeat, and who would go on fighting until he died on his feet.

Once Mulvane caught a glimpse of the

Countess Hannau. She had pushed up somewhat closer and was watching the fight, wide-brimmed hat pulled down on her head, arms folded across her breasts.

Once again Von Dreber nearly caught Mulvane. For the first time the Prussian got his hands on his man, one hand on Mulvane's neck, and the other around his waist, as he tried to draw Mulvane in toward him.

Mulvane ripped a fist in under Von Dreber's chin as he was being pulled in, and as the Prussian's head jerked back he tore himself loose. It had been close that time, though, and the crowd let out a low hum of excitement. Mulvane was beginning to realize that it was only a matter of time now before Von Dreber closed with him, and when that happened the fight would be over. He knew very definitely that he could not hope to match Von Dreber's terrible strength.

Von Dreber still plodded after him, very patient, making no sounds, even though his face was a bloodied pulp now with one bright blue eye gleaming out of the mass of ripped flesh.

It was the most discouraging free-for-all fight Mulvane had ever had in his life. There seemed to be no stopping the man, no slowing him down. Von Dreber, despite the fact that he'd been hit a hundred times—heavy, slogging blows—had not even been knocked off his feet, and Mulvane's hands were bruised and puffed. The time would shortly come when he would be unable to strike Von Dreber with those hands. In Von Dreber's single good eye he saw the gleam of triumph. This was apparently the way Von Dreber had expected the fight to go, and he was confident now of winning.

They had been fighting for fully twenty minutes when Von Dreber finally got a firm grip on Mulvane. Trying to elude Von Dreber's clutching hands Mulvane backed into the tie rack nearby, and before he could jump clear Von Dreber had both arms around his waist and was drawing him back toward the center of the circle.

Desperately, Mulvane tried to break loose. He rammed his fists hard up into Von Dreber's face but the German was holding him close now and he could get no leverage behind his blows. Von Dreber had him in the dreaded bear hug, big hands knotted into the small of Mulvane's back as he gradually squeezed the breath out of him.

As Von Dreber finally got his grip a low, almost mournful sigh, swept through the crowd. A woman who had been watching from a house window let out a short, terrified scream.

Again and again Mulvane slashed at Von Dreber's bloodied face but the blows had no effect whatever now. The Prussian increased the pressure, burying his head into Mulvane's shoulder. His arms felt like iron bands around

Mulvane's body as he tightened and tightened some more.

Frantically, Mulvane fought for his breath even though he knew it was a losing fight. He had beaten Von Dreber horribly, beaten him more than he'd beaten any man in his life, but the German was still strong, still indomitable.

Even as he beat at Von Dreber's torn face his eyes were becoming blurred. The street lights were dancing crazily. He could not breathe. His arms felt limp at his sides.

Then he felt his back on the ground and his body was pressed into the dust of the road by Von Dreber's weight. Strong fingers dug deep into his throat. He had one thought as the darkness closed in over him: that it was a hell of a way to die!

CHAPTER 12

After a while he could hear voices. Joe Smith was talking, and the gunman was saying casually, "Reckon he's comin' around now."

Mulvane opened his eyes and found himself in the back room of the El Dorado. Joe and Bill Smith were there, along with one of the bartenders. Outside in the main room he could hear the noise.

Joe Smith said dryly, "You're still alive, Mulvane. I ain't no damned angel."

Mulvane nodded. He felt of his throat with his fingers and he swallowed, feeling the pain. He remembered that Von Dreber had been deliberately, coolly choking him to death.

"What happened?" he asked.

"I bent the barrel of my gun over the Dutchman's skull," Joe Smith grinned. "Had to hit him twice, too, before it got through."

Bill Smith said casually, "You hit him hard enough so's he'll have a headache for a month."

"Ain't no way to kill a man with your hands," Joe Smith observed. "We don't do it that way in this country."

Mulvane again swallowed, and then Joe Smith handed him a liquor glass. The bartender stood by, bottle and glass in hand, watching them.

"Drink her down," Joe Smith told him. "Might make your throat feel better."

"Where's Von Dreber now?" Mulvane wanted to know.

"Couple of 'em carried him to the hotel," Joe Smith said. "They got Doc Andrews over there. You sure made him a sight before he got that bear hug on you." He added, "Reckon there's not a man in the country kin beat him down. His kind just don't go down. They stand up till they're dead."

Mulvane downed the drink and he said, "Obliged. Reckon you know Von Dreber will be after your scalp from now on."

The gunman shrugged. "After yours, too," he observed, "but he ain't got it, yet."

It was fully thirty minutes before Mulvane felt strong enough to stand up and go outside. He was still weak, though, and his ribs were tender. The floorman standing at the foot of the stairs said as he came out, "Miss Elder would like to see you, Mr. Mulvane."

He saw Trasker Flynn angling across the floor toward him, and he waited before going up the steps. Flynn said as he came up, "Told you he was a bad one, Mulvane. You don't fight that kind with your fists."

"I tried," Mulvane said.

Trasker Flynn said almost reluctantly, "He'll

want me to go after you now, Mulvane. Reckon you know that."

Mulvane nodded. "Your job," he said.

"If I come," Flynn told him, "it'll be out front. You won't have to worry about the alleys."

"Figured that," Mulvane nodded again, and he went on up the stairs to Rosslyn Elder's room.

She was sitting up when he came in, and she had coffee ready for him.

"You were a fool," she said as he sat down, "but then most men are fools. He wouldn't come at you with a gun. Why did you give him the satisfaction of trying to fight him with your hands?"

"Like to give every man satisfaction," Mulvane smiled, "even the devil."

"You're lucky to be alive," Rosslyn said severely. "I watched it from the window."

"Did you?" Mulvane mused.

"He wouldn't have killed you," Rosslyn Elder said, "even if your man hadn't stepped in with his gun."

Mulvane looked at her, eyebrows lifted.

"I had a rifle on him from this window," Rosslyn said coolly. "I would have pulled the trigger in another moment."

Mulvane sipped his coffee, and the hot liquid felt good on his throat. "Reckon I didn't know I was so well protected," he said. "Friends come in handy. I'm obliged."

"You know how I feel about you," Rosslyn said, and Mulvane frowned.

"You can find a better man," he told her, "a man without pebbles in his boots."

"I pick my own men," Rosslyn smiled, "and I like them to be alive."

"You don't want me to run from Von Dreber," Mulvane said. "You tried to sign me up to buck him."

"Not that way," Rosslyn said. "Not with your bare hands; not out in the middle of the road."

Mulvane looked at her over the coffee cup. "I fight a man the way I damned please," he said softly, "not the way a woman tells me to fight him."

Rosslyn sighed. "I should have expected that," she said. "I shouldn't have said it."

"You shouldn't have said it," Mulvane agreed, and he let the matter drop.

"What's your next play up at O'Leary's?" Rosslyn asked.

"We sit tight," Mulvane told her, "and we play it close to the vest. Sooner or later that crowd behind Von Dreber will begin to realize that he can be whipped. Then they'll drop away from him. He's the power right now in this country."

"What if he tries to run stock on the ranges which have been vacated?"

"I'll drive him off," Mulvane said evenly.

Rosslyn Elder smiled. "I never thought I'd hear

anybody speak like that about Von Dreber," she said. "I'm glad you're fighting with us."

After a while Mulvane went downstairs, and as he was crossing the saloon floor, searching for the Smiths, the bellboy from the hotel handed him a note.

Stepping outside on the porch, Mulvane read it from the light of the window. It was from the Countess Hannau and she was asking him to meet her at the rear stable behind the hotel. There was nothing suspicious about the note. Mulvane recognized it as a woman's handwriting, and there was even the faint odor of perfume about the paper.

Slipping the note into his shirt pocket he stepped down to the walk and headed up in the direction of the hotel. If what Joe Smith had told him was true, Von Dreber wouldn't be leaving the hotel room until morning or perhaps later than that.

It was past nine o'clock in the evening as Mulvane headed up the street toward the hotel. Moving past the Wyoming Saloon, he saw Neil McAdams just inside the door, his sweaty face flushed with drink. Outside the hotel he caught a glimpse of Hans Krauss, Von Dreber's valet and servant, standing near the door. Krauss didn't see him as he turned down the alley to the stables.

Countess Hannau was waiting just to the left of the open stable door, standing in the shadow, a tall, slender woman in riding clothes. She put a hand on his arm when he came up and said in a low voice, "I was not sure you would come, Herr Mulvane."

"I'm here," Mulvane said. "How is Von Dreber?"

"Badly hurt," the Countess informed him. "The doctor says he should not leave the room for twenty-four hours at least." She added, "You beat him terribly."

"He damn near killed me," Mulvane observed dryly. "I'm lucky to be alive." He looked down at her, seeing her oval face in the dim starlight. She was looking up at him, her eyes wide and warm.

"You are wondering why I sent to see you, Herr Mulvane?" she said.

"Reckon I'm wondering," Mulvane nodded. "You came over here to marry Von Dreber, and I'm no friend of Von Dreber's."

The Countess Hannau looked at him steadily, and then she said, "I am not too pleased with what I have found in this country. I had been led to believe that Colonel Von Dreber had secured a large tract of land and already had a sizeable following of disciples in this country."

"You found that you'd gotten yourself into a hornet's nest," Mulvane said. "You found that the people over here aren't being pushed around."

"This was the wrong place for the experiment," Hilda Hannau went on. "It has been a great mistake."

"The smart thing for Von Dreber to do," Mulvane observed, "is to pull up stakes and get out of this country." Even as he said it, though, he knew that Kurt Von Dreber would never do this in a million years. He'd built his stone castle on the hill, and he was here to stay. Remembering how Von Dreber had fought him in the street this evening, he realized that there was little chance of the Prussian pulling out.

"He will never go," Hilda Hannau said.

"What about you?"

"I have told the Colonel I thought he would be more successful in his own country with his own people." The Countess was looking straight at him now. She said, "I have decided to return to Prussia and continue our work there even if Colonel Von Dreber stays."

Mulvane looked at her, and then took his tobacco sack from his shirt pocket and started to roll a cigarette. "What do you want from me?" he asked.

"I am prepared to make an offer to you," the Countess told him. "I can make you wealthy for the remainder of your life. Return with me to Prussia."

Mulvane stared. "Reckon I don't believe what you believe," he pointed out.

The Countess shook her head impatiently. "It does not matter," she told him. "I have a large estate in Prussia, and many holdings. I can begin the movement alone but I need a man at my side, a man such as you, Herr Mulvane."

Mulvane got his smoke going and leaned back against the wall of the barn. He pushed his hat back on his head. "You're buying me?" he asked softly.

The Countess shook her head again. "Call it what you wish," she said. "I can start east and arrange to meet you in Chicago. No one would ever know." She would have said more, but Mulvane was shaking his head slowly.

"Reckon I like this country," he said. "I don't aim to leave it."

The Countess Hannau said nothing for several long moments as she stood looking at him. Then she said slowly, evenly, "You like another woman, do you not? The woman from the saloon?"

"There's no other woman," Mulvane said. "I don't figure on leaving this country."

"You lie!" Hilda Hannau hissed. "If you were in my country I would have you horsewhipped now."

"I'm damned lucky that I'm not in your country," Mulvane smiled. He pushed away from the wall and said, "In this country, or any country, I hope your movement fails. Your whole plan is rotten. You try to make men less than animals, and it won't work."

He started to walk away, but Hilda Hannau caught his arm, stopping him. Her voice was vibrant with anger now, and she spoke with a more pronounced German accent.

"You are a fool, Herr Mulvane," she grated. "Do you think I will let you just walk away from here and go to another woman? I will stay now; I will stay with Colonel Von Dreber, and together we shall destroy you. I do not care about these other fools. It is you I want to see hurt, dragged down from that big horse you ride."

"I'll take a hell of a lot of dragging," Mulvane told her. He walked off, leaving her standing at the corner of the barn.

He started to walk away, but Hilda Hannau caught his arm, moved back toward the El Dorado. The talk with Countess Hannau had not been particularly pleasant, and he realized that he'd made an enemy who very possibly could be even more vindictive than Von Dreber, himself.

Neil McAdams was standing on the walk out in front of the Wyoming Saloon. As Mulvane came down the walk McAdams flipped a stub of cigar across his path and said insolently, "Damned lucky to be alive, aren't you, Mulvane?"

Mulvane pulled up, jaw tight. "You have anything to say to me, McAdams," he snapped, "say it and get the hell out of the way."

"I'll say it," McAdams grinned. "In a week we'll have your damned rag-tail band of rustlers off O'Leary's spread and we'll be doing it legally, too."

Mulvane saw a gleam of triumph in the lawman's bleary eyes. Drunk, McAdams was unable to keep his secret to himself, whatever it was.

"How legal?" Mulvane asked, hoping McAdams would keep his tongue going. "O'Leary has title to his place."

He remembered turning up in Wickburg only a few months after little Charlie O'Leary, for the first time in his life, had settled down to run stock on a spread of his own. He remembered Charlie showing him the deed he'd gotten from the homesteader who'd owned the land previously. Charlie had been quite proud of that piece of paper.

"Title, hell," McAdams laughed. "We've got proof the homesteader he bought it from never proved up on it. That land is back in the public domain, which means anybody can use it, water rights and all."

Mulvane frowned at the fat-faced lawman, but he had little doubt that McAdams was telling the truth this time. It was going to be a tough blow to Charlie O'Leary.

"And he's not the only one, either," McAdams went on tersely. "We have a lawyer working on these claims, and I wouldn't be surprised if half of your crowd loses legal title to their spreads before we're finished."

"You can take this from me," Mulvane told him quietly, "and from all the other ranchers up at O'Leary's spread. Don't come out there until you're mighty sure you're right."

"I'll be sure," McAdams laughed sardonically.

Mulvane moved by him, heading toward the El Dorado. It was another half-block to the gambling house, and he had to pass a narrow alley between a saddlemaker's shop and an abandoned store. After the talk with Hilda Hannau and Neil McAdams Mulvane was momentarily off guard, forgetting that even though he'd shot down one of the three men Von Dreber had sent after him, there were still two left, and the chances were that they'd be going for his back.

Coming abreast of the alley, he would have given it no concern had he not caught the dull glint of gunmetal back in the shadows. The alley was dark, but starlight filtered down.

He was moving, therefore, when the gun boomed, orange flame reaching out toward him from the alley at a distance of less than fifteen feet. The quick step saved his life. The lead touched his right sleeve as he stepped to his right.

He was bringing his gun from the holster when the rifle cracked from across the road, the slug slamming through the window of the abandoned store just a few inches above his head.

The two Smiths had been lounging on the porch of the El Dorado waiting for him, and he heard

Joe Smith yell as he hit the walk. As Mulvane tore into the alley, gun in hand, he could hear a man moving toward the other end, stumbling over refuse there.

He sent one shot after the runner and took off after the man. The two bushwhackers had had him set up this time very neatly from the alley and from one of the houses across the street, and he was fortunate to be alive.

Reaching the far end of the alley he stopped, listening, not quite sure whether the killer had gone to the right or to the left. Then he heard a door close off to his right, and he took off in that direction, vaulting over a low, rickety wood fence, and swinging around the rear of a stable. Beyond the stable was a rear door, which if he gauged himself correctly, would be the back of the Wyoming Saloon.

Pushing through the door, Mulvane found himself in a rear storeroom filled with empty or full beer kegs. In the dim light he moved toward a lighted crack which he took to be a doorway. Opening it, he found himself in a hallway which opened on the saloon proper.

It was only a few steps into the saloon and Mulvane stepped into the room, hand on his gun. The Wyoming Saloon was nearly empty. The single bartender stood behind the bar, both hands on the counter, looking straight at him as he came in through the door. Three men sat at a card game near one wall. Two other men were at the bar. One man had his back toward Mulvane; the second fellow faced him and he was drunk, reeling slightly as he stood at the bar, glass in hand. He was a thin-faced, blond man with a mustache, his face red with drink.

Mulvane stared at the men in the saloon, all of whom were looking at him. The drinker who'd had his back turned, swung around, also, giving him a cold stare, and then went back to his drinking.

The way they were looking at him convinced Mulvane that a man had just come through here and they were going to cover up for him. The bartender, a stout man with a brush of black mustache, stared at Mulvane and then at his hand on the gun.

It was the drunk who gave it away. The drunk looked at Mulvane stupidly, and then his vacant blue eyes moved toward a door to the right of the bar which evidently led to a back room.

There was an overturned beer keg standing just to the right of the door. Mulvane stepped up to the keg softly, picked it up, and hurled it through the door, smashing it open. He went into the room, then, gun in hand, seeing Jug Streiber sitting against the wall ten feet away, a card table in front of him, his sixgun resting on the rim of the table. Streiber had his hat pushed back on his flaxen hair and an expression of dazed surprise on his face as Mulvane's bullet struck him in the chest.

Streiber still retained his grip on the sixgun, but now the muzzle of the gun was pointing toward the ceiling. It went off with a roar, the lead ripping through the plaster ceiling, sending a tiny shower of white dust down on the table top in front of him.

Very slowly Streiber's body slid down, his hat rubbing against the wall behind him, covering his face. When Strieber had slid all the way down to the floor and out of sight behind the table, Mulvane turned and walked out of the room, holstering his gun as he did so.

The bartender had come over to have a look and he said tersely, "Hell of a lot o' killings around here lately. You brought in that Blassingame tonight, didn't you, mister?"

"I brought him in," Mulvane nodded. He motioned to the room behind him, "And this one opened on me tonight from an alley. McAdams saw it, himself."

He walked out of the saloon, then, and reaching the street he saw the two Smiths standing near the opening to the alley. Both men had their guns drawn.

"Heard a shot," Joe Smith said succinctly.

"One of them's dead," Mulvane told him. "What about the other one?"

"Skipped pretty fast," Bill Smith explained.

"We found where he was waitin' for you in the house across the way. He had a horse out back."

Joe Smith said, "Another one of Von Dreber's boys?"

Mulvane nodded.

"You keep gunnin' 'em down," Joe Smith grinned, "an' there'll be no more damned war around here."

Neil McAdams now came toward them from the direction of the El Dorado. He said sourly, "Who in hell threw the shot?"

The man had been less than fifteen feet away when Streiber had fired at Mulvane from the alley, and he'd undoubtedly heard the shot and he'd seen Mulvane take off into the alley. He'd made no attempt to follow him, though.

"Strieber threw lead at me," Mulvane told him, and then when McAdams waited, he added, "Find him in the Wyoming."

McAdams mumbled something under his breath and then walked toward the Wyoming Saloon. Joe Smith said, "One hell of a night, Mulvane. Reckon we'd better get back to camp."

Mulvane nodded. As they were riding out of Wickburg a few minutes later Bill Smith said thoughtfully, "Kind of glad you're ridin' with us, Mulvane. You damn near didn't."

Mulvane smiled faintly, remembering Von Dreber's ironlike grip on his back and then his throat, remembering, also, the bullet Jug Streiber had fired at him from the alley, and the additional shot from across the road. He'd been lucky this night, and he wondered how long this luck would hold out!

CHAPTER 13

At mid-morning the next day Neil McAdams rode out from Wickburg with a lawyer, a small, thin-faced, bespectacled man in black with a string tie and a button of a nose.

Charlie O'Leary said curiously as the two riders came into sight, "Reckon that's Jason Phipps, the lawyer."

Mulvane had not told him as yet of McAdams' threats, and he decided to wait now to see what the lawman had to say. The two men dismounted near the line shack, McAdams looking around distastefully at the men scattered nearby.

Charlie O'Leary said softly, "Come to put me off my land, Sheriff?"

"We'll get to that soon enough," McAdams told him. "Mr. Phipps here would like to see the deed you have for this land, O'Leary."

Charlie was grinning. "Figure you got me there, don't you, Sheriff?" he chuckled. "When that fire burned me out you figured the deed to this place was burned, too. Had it buried in a tin box under the floor."

Jason Phipps said rather crisply, "I'd like to see the deed, please."

Mulvane said to the lawyer, "On whose authority?"

"Mine," McAdams snapped. "As sheriff of this county. There has been a question as to the legality of this piece of property. I'm here to investigate."

"Hell," Charlie O'Leary grinned, "I got the deed, Mulvane. There's nothin' to worry about."

Mulvane frowned as he watched Charlie O'Leary duck into the shack and come out in a few moments with a small metal box. He produced the deed and turned it over to the lawyer.

"All legal-like," Charlie said. "It was drawn up by Old Man Catby, best lawyer in these parts till he drank hisself to death."

Phipps said after a cursory examination, "Everything appears to be in order. I see you purchased the property from a man by the name of Moorhead, Abe Moorhead."

Charlie O'Leary nodded. "Sodbuster went broke tryin' to farm range country. This is cattle land. Good grass; good water, maybe the best in the country."

"Moorhead was a homesteader?" Jason Phipps asked.

"Sodbuster," Charlie nodded.

"And that meant that he had to prove up on his land before he had legal title to it. Is that right, Mr. O'Leary?"

Charlie O'Leary's blue eyes flicked, and for the first time the smile disappeared from his face. "Reckon I don't know too damned much about that Homestead Act, mister, but the land is mine. I bought it with good, solid cash."

"It is yours," Jason Phipps informed him coldly, "if Mr. Moorhead had legal title to the property, and was therefore in a position to sell. According to the records Abraham Moorhead never proved up on his land. He'd lived here less than four years before he sold it to you, and during that time he hadn't farmed the land consecutively."

Charlie O'Leary was staring now. "What the hell does that mean?" he snapped.

"It means that Moorhead had no right to sell his property to you," Phipps went on calmly, "and therefore the title is null and void. The land automatically goes back into the public domain."

"The hell it does!" Charlie spluttered.

The other ranchers had gathered around and were listening in amazement. Ben Meigs said now, "Sounds like a cheap lawyer trick to me. Moorhead was a good man. I knew him well before you came to this country, Charlie."

Jason Phipps said evenly, "Was Mr. Moorhead here for the full five years?"

Meigs scowled. "Damned if I know if he was here five years," he said, "but he farmed this place. That I know. It just didn't pay off."

Neil McAdams said, a gleam of triumph in his eyes, "Figured you boys might like to know this piece of property has been checked and this land will shortly go back into the public domain, which means that you'd better get this stock to hell out of here."

"Where can we take it," Meigs snapped, "where you and your sniveling lawyer friend won't come around and try to push us again?"

Charlie O'Leary said quietly, his face pale with anger, "My land, McAdams. I'm stayin'. Anybody tries to put me off had better come with a gun."

McAdams said cheerfully, "I can get a whole damned troop of cavalry to put you off when I'm ready."

Mulvane spoke for the first time. He said, "You'll need a hell of a lot more proof than you've got now, McAdams."

Phipps said, "If you'll check at the land office in Metropolitan City you will discover that Mr. Abraham Moorhead farmed this property less than four years."

Mulvane looked down at his boot tips and then he said, "The law states that a homesteader can sell his property after six months for a dollar and a quarter an acre if he can prove that he cultivated it during that time."

Jason Phipps was frowning at him.

Mulvane said to Charlie O'Leary, "You figure you paid at least a dollar and a quarter an acre for your rangeland, Charlie?"

"Damned right," Charlie grinned. "Closer to

double that. An' still it wasn't much. I got the best water in this country."

Mulvane said to the lawyer, "Up to you to prove that Abe Moorhead didn't cultivate this property for six months."

McAdams said tersely, "We'll prove it, mister, and we'll prove it on a lot more of these damned rustlers' ranges."

Mulvane said two words to him. He said, "Ride out."

Casually, Joe Smith took his sixgun from the holster and pointed the muzzle at Jason Phipps' stomach. He said easily, "You, too, tin-horn."

The little lawyer rode off hastily, followed by Neil McAdams. After they were gone, Charlie O'Leary wiped his face with a bandanna and said, "Hell of a business, Mulvane. You figure they can cause us trouble?"

Mulvane nodded soberly. "Easy enough," he stated. "McAdams can bribe plenty of people around here to swear that Moorhead never cultivated the land."

"I knew Moorhead for two years," Meigs growled. "He worked the land. I'll swear to that."

"Reckon we'll worry about it when McAdams makes a play," Mulvane said. "Could be he was just bluffing. I don't figure Von Dreber is too anxious to have government troopers come in here, either."

• • •

It was high noon when Charlie O'Leary hitched up his buckboard to ride into town for supplies, taking Bill Smith with him. Mulvane watched them move off, O'Leary on the seat of the buckboard, and Bill Smith riding his chestnut gelding in the rear.

It was four o'clock in the afternoon when Charlie returned alone, face pale, and obviously quite shaken. Mulvane had taken a short ride in the direction of Von Dreber's castle to see if any of the swastika brand stock had moved over on to Charlie's range. He was unsaddling the claybank when Charlie pulled the buckboard up a few yards away.

Mulvane looked at him and then down the trace toward town, wondering if Bill Smith were coming on behind. Charlie swallowed and then said in a low voice, "Reckon we just lost a pretty good man, Mulvane."

Mulvane looked at him across the rump of the claybank. He saw Joe Smith coming over, curiosity in his pale blue eyes.

"Lost a man?" Mulvane repeated.

"Smith," Charlie O'Leary said.

"Run out?" Joe Smith asked incredulously.

Charlie shook his head. "Reckon Trasker Flynn gunned him down," he said as he stared down at the ground. When Mulvane didn't say anything he went on in a low voice, "Went into the El Dorado for a drink while I was stockin' up. Fair fight they told me. Smith had his gun and it was out o' the holster when Flynn's bullet got him."

Without a word Joe Smith hoisted his saddle to his shoulder and started walking toward the tethered horses nearby. Mulvane called, "Hold it up."

Joe Smith stopped and looked back at him.

"What was the fight about, Charlie?" Mulvane asked quietly.

O'Leary shrugged. "Nobody seems to know. They had a few words at the bar and then Bill Smith pulled his gun. He didn't pull it fast enough. Not many of 'em kin slap leather with Trasker Flynn. One shot an' it was over."

Mulvane turned and walked over to where Joe Smith was waiting. "Going to town?" he asked.

"You know it," Joe Smith nodded, lean face hard. "Reckon I kind o' liked Bill."

Mulvane said, "This might be what Flynn wants. He'll be playing for us one at a time."

"An' he'll get his chance," Joe Smith nodded. "Never yet saw the man could scare me out of a draw, Mulvane."

Mulvane said, "He'll kill you."

"Maybe so," Joe Smith smiled faintly, "but I'm damned curious to find out."

Mulvane had no argument to this. He said briefly, "Saddle up. I'll ride with you."

"You don't have to," Joe Smith objected.

"You didn't have to last night, either," Mulvane said. "I'll ride in."

He went back to Charlie O'Leary, who was still sitting up on the seat, a frown on his face. "Flynn still in town?" he asked.

"Was when I left," Charlie said, and then he shook his head as if puzzled. "Had it figured all along," he said. "Flynn wasn't takin' part in this fight even though he'd signed up with Von Dreber. You figure Von Dreber put the pressure on him after last night?"

Mulvane shook his head. He'd been quite surprised, himself, as Flynn had given him every indication that he had no heart for this particular range war and was only marking time until he could pull out of it. He wondered idly if the fight had been simply a disagreement between Trasker Flynn and Bill Smith. The two men had known each other previously and today may have settled an ancient quarrel.

They rode into Wickburg an hour later, dismounting in front of the El Dorado. Wickburg's single straggling street was nearly deserted this late afternoon hour with the sun glinting red on the windows facing west. Here and there a horse stood at a tie rack. There was a buckboard out in front of the General Store.

The El Dorado was nearly empty as they went inside. Two men stood at the bar drinking in solitary fashion. A card game was going on in the corner. The floorman came down the stairs and spotted Mulvane at the bar. He crossed over, shoes squeaking as he walked.

Mulvane said to him, "You saw the fight?"

The floorman nodded. "That damned Flynn is greased lightning with a gun. It was a fair enough fight. Your man started his draw but he wasn't quick enough."

"Know what it was about?" Mulvane asked him.

The floorman shook his head. "Men die in this damned town every other day," he said, "an' never a reason for it."

Mulvane was surprised now to see Rosslyn Elder coming down the stairs. He was sure it was the first time she'd made an appearance since the beating. There were still a few cuts on her face, but aside from that she seemed to be all right.

She was not smiling as she greeted Mulvane, and she said, "I expected you."

"My rider was shot and killed," Mulvane told her. "Man has a right to find out why."

"You know why," Rosslyn said tersely. "Flynn is one of Von Dreber's hired killers. His job is to cut you all down."

Mulvane didn't say anything to this. He said, "Flynn ride out?"

The floorman who was still standing nearby

shook his head. "Last I saw him he was up at the hotel. Von Dreber hasn't left the hotel as yet, and that woman is with him."

Joe Smith said, "We'd better be goin', Mulvane. He won't stay around here forever."

Rosslyn Elder said, "I suppose you have to see him."

"We have to see him," Mulvane nodded. "I figure it might have been a personal matter between him and our rider."

"I wouldn't count on it," Rosslyn said. She added soberly, "I understand he's very dangerous."

Mulvane nodded. "Fastest man in the country with a gun," he said.

The floorman looked at him. "Faster than you?" he asked.

Mulvane smiled. "He's faster than I am."

This time Joe Smith looked at him curiously. They went outside and turned up the walk in the direction of the hotel. As they were going up the street Joe Smith said, "You figure he's faster than you with a gun?"

"He's faster," Mulvane admitted, and then he added without emotion, "I've killed men before who were faster than I am."

Before they reached the hotel Trasker Flynn came out through the front door. He was not alone, though. The Countess Hannau walked with him. She was wearing a pink dress with

173

white ruffles this afternoon, and she was a vision of beauty with her golden hair, her perfect complexion, and her blue eyes.

As they came down the walk she was chatting gayly with Trasker Flynn, giving him her undivided attention. The little gunman walked beside her, a trifle shorter than she, and obviously quite taken by the Countess's attentions.

Mulvane and Joe Smith stood to one side as the couple approached. Seeing them, Trasker Flynn slowed down, the smile leaving his face momentarily. Hilda Hannau saw them, also, and she looked straight at Mulvane, her mouth suddenly tight. He saw the malice in her eyes.

Flynn said, "You boys want to see me?"

Mulvane nodded. "We lost a rider this afternoon, Trasker. Our man cross you up?"

Flynn smiled, revealing his white teeth. There was no particular expression in his dark brown eyes. He fingered the gold watch chain hanging from his vest and said, "You might say he crossed me up, Mulvane. He made some statements to which I took exception."

Mulvane nodded.

"Man in my position," Trasker Flynn observed, "cannot take slights, Mulvane. One does it and they all do it, and then I'm dead. You know that."

Mulvane nodded again. He glanced at Hilda Hannau and he saw the hatred in her eyes, and now he understood. He touched his hat to the woman and then he stepped back, letting them pass on.

When they were out of hearing Joe Smith said, "He lied like hell. I couldn't call him, though, with a woman on his arm."

Mulvane didn't say anything to this. He, too, was convinced that Trasker Flynn had lied, and now he understood why Flynn had shot down Bill Smith, and why Flynn would go after all of them now, one by one. Colonel Von Dreber had not been able to bring Trasker Flynn into this fight, even though he'd paid money. The Countess Hannau was doing it her own way.

"He'll go for me next," Joe Smith mused. "Or O'Leary. Then he'll want you. After that there'll be no more war."

Mulvane turned and watched Flynn step into a ladies' hat store with the Countess Hannau.

"How fast is he?" Joe Smith asked softly.

"Faster than you," Mulvane told him.

"And you never saw me," Joe Smith reminded him.

"I've seen your kind," Mulvane smiled. "He's faster."

"Have to show it to me," Joe Smith mused, and Mulvane knew how it was with men of this calibre. There was always the streak of curiosity running through them. They had to know, and they could not sleep until they knew, and when they knew sometimes they were dead and it didn't matter anyway!

CHAPTER 14

Joe Smith was saying as they moved down the walk, "We stay in this town until one or the other braces him?"

Mulvane shook his head. He said, "What if Bill Smith did say something out of turn and was asking to be killed?"

Joe Smith put his back up against one of the awning uprights and rubbed himself gently. He said in a low voice, "You're not afraid of him, Mulvane?"

Mulvane scowled. "Trasker Flynn was a friend of mine," he said.

"And he picked his fight with one of our riders," Joe Smith said, "and shot him dead. We ride out of this town without doing anything about it and we're telling everybody that there's a new rider on the high seat. Reckon you don't want that and I don't want it."

"There's time," Mulvane tried to tell him. "We'll watch Flynn for his next move."

"Not me," Joe Smith said promptly.

Mulvane looked at him. "You ride for this outfit," he said, "and you take orders."

"Fire me," Joe Smith said cheerfully. "I'm staying in town tonight, Mulvane." He pushed his hat back on his head, then, and crossed the street to the Frontier Saloon, disappearing inside.

Mulvane stared after the man for a moment, and then he walked up the street to where they had tied the two horses and led them down the alley to the Ace High Livery.

Night was falling as he came out of the alley and crossed to the restaurant for his supper. It was fully dark and he was finishing his supper as he saw Von Dreber's buckboard go by with Von Dreber and Hilda Hannau on the seat, and the valet, Krauss, riding in the rear. Von Dreber was leaving when it was dark so the people of this town couldn't see his battered, misshapen face.

Mulvane sat at the table finishing his cigar, a frown on his face. Unsuccessfully, he tried to convince himself that Trasker Flynn had had to shoot Bill Smith because of an affront. He knew deep down in his heart, though, that the Countess Hannau had worked her way into Flynn's confidence and she'd persuaded him that Mulvane had to die. What she'd promised Flynn for this he could only imagine.

Mulvane was remembering one occasion when he'd gone fishing with Trasker Flynn many years ago. He remembered the huge delight the little gunman had displayed because he'd caught more trout than his fishing companion. They'd stood by each other with guns in those days. Now it seemed only a matter of time before they reversed those guns.

Sitting at his table and looking out through the window, Mulvane saw Joe Smith angling across the street toward the El Dorado. Watching him, Mulvane almost felt sorry for the man. Out of sheer curiosity Smith had to match guns with another man. This was the difference between the professional gunhand and himself.

After paying for the meal Mulvane stepped outside, hesitated, and then crossed over to the El Dorado. Joe Smith had taken a seat at one of the card games, sitting in such a position that he could watch the front door.

Trasker Flynn was not in the room, but Mulvane remembered that the little gunman had not ridden out with Von Dreber, which meant that he was still in town, and it would only be a matter of time before he crossed Joe Smith's path.

There was a faint smile on Joe Smith's face as he watched Mulvane cross the floor toward the far end of the bar where Rosslyn Elder was standing watching him.

"You didn't ride out," Rosslyn said. "I noticed your horse was gone and I'd thought you'd decided to go back to camp."

"Not yet," Mulvane said. He looked again in Joe Smith's direction and Rosslyn frowned. She said, "Why does he want to get himself killed?"

"Why does anybody?" Mulvane countered.

"We've never seen a man like Flynn before in this town," Rosslyn said.

"I've seen him," Mulvane said.

"Now stay out of it," Rosslyn warned. "If your fool rider wants to get his head shot off that's his business."

"He rides for me," Mulvane reminded her. "If Flynn picks this fight I'm in it."

Neil McAdams came into the room, a satisfied look on his face. Seeing Mulvane he walked toward the other end of the bar.

"You want to give him the satisfaction of seeing you carried out of here?" Rosslyn asked.

"They're not carrying me out," Mulvane smiled. Then he signaled for the bartender. He was engaged in conversation with the floorman when Trasker Flynn came into the establishment an hour later. The little gunman pushed in through the bat-wing doors, a half smile on his face.

Flynn had one drink at the bar, chatting genially with the bartender, one elbow resting on the wood as his brown eyes moved over the room, pausing for one moment on Mulvane near the stairway, and then passing on to stop upon Joe Smith still at the card table. Flynn was smiling this evening, but it was a different kind of smile. His eyes seemed to be lighter in color.

Finishing his drink, Flynn moved over to where Neil McAdams was standing and they had a few words. McAdams then left the saloon. Still standing with the floorman, Mulvane watched Joe Smith get up from his chair at the card table, and then leisurely cross to the bar to cash in his chips.

At the far end of the bar Flynn was pouring himself a drink, apparently unconcerned, but Mulvane was convinced that the gunman was watching Joe Smith carefully.

As Joe Smith pushed away from the bar and moved in Flynn's direction, hitching at his gunbelt as he did so, Mulvane stepped away from the floorman. Flynn turned to face Joe Smith as he came up. He was smiling quite pleasantly as he looked up at the taller gunman.

Watching them, Mulvane realized that there was nothing he could do now. This was the way Joe Smith wanted it and this was the way he would have it, and nothing on earth could stop it.

The words they were speaking to each other were mockery. This was just the preliminary to the gunfire both men knew was shortly forthcoming. The bartender who had been nearest to them now started to move away. Two drinkers at the bar left their drinks and headed in the direction of the door.

Now Joe Smith started to back away, a half-smile on his face, the big gun on his hip clear. Flynn stayed where he was, his left elbow still resting on the bar, black coat open, the Navy Colt he wore clear.

Men along the bar seeing Joe Smith moving back hastily pulled out of the way. A chair went down as a card player left his seat precipitously.

"All right," Joe Smith said in a loud voice.

Trasker Flynn was still smiling, revealing the even white teeth beneath the black mustache. It was Smith who drew his gun first. The blond gunman's right hand dropped toward the butt of the gun on his hip, and at the same time he moved toward his left.

This slight maneuver saved his life. Before Smith's Colt gun had cleared the holster Trasker Flynn's bullet struck him in the right shoulder, spinning him half-around.

Surprise in his blue eyes, Joe Smith kept trying to pull the gun out of the holster, but there was no strength in his right arm now. Flynn had the big Navy Colt lined on the target and was ready to squeeze the trigger when Mulvane said sharply, "Trasker."

He had his own gun out, leveled on Flynn's chest, very steady in his hand. Flynn, who had not moved from his position at the bar, turned his head to look at Mulvane, his brown eyes dropping to the gun in Mulvane's hand. He shrugged slightly and slipped the Navy back into the holster.

Joe Smith, shock and incredulity still showing on his face, reached out with his left hand to grab at the bar to support himself. He stood there looking down at the wood and then he shook his head as if in disgust at himself.

Mulvane walked up and said quietly, "Can you walk?"

"Damned lucky if I can," Joe Smith scowled.

Flynn came up then and said almost apologetically, "The man made some remarks, Mulvane."

Mulvane nodded.

"I called him out," Joe Smith admitted. He stood at the bar still supporting himself with his left hand, lips drawn tight in pain now.

"I can't let a man call me out," Trasker Flynn observed. "Can I now, Mulvane?"

Mulvane just looked at him. "A hell of a lot of men are calling you out these days," he said, and Flynn nodded soberly.

"It's a rough town," Flynn said, and he adjusted his hat and walked off, going out through the batwing doors.

Rosslyn Elder came up and said quietly, "Can I do anything, Mulvane?"

Mulvane shook his head. "I'll get him to the doctor's," he said, and he put an arm around Joe Smith's waist and started him toward the door. As they went out into the cool of the night Joe Smith said slowly, "Reckon I'm damned lucky to be alive, Mulvane."

"You're lucky," Mulvane agreed.

"He's too damned fast for anybody alive," Joe Smith mused. "I don't know where in hell that gun came from."

"He's used it before," Mulvane observed dryly.

He sat in the doctor's office while the physician extracted the bullet and bound up the wound.

"How bad?" he asked.

The doctor, a short, balding man with spectacles, dropped the lead pellet into a trash basket and said, "He won't use that gun hand for a month or so. Aside from that he'll be all right."

Joe Smith lay on the table staring up at the ceiling, face drawn. He said as Mulvane helped him up, "Damned if I know how he got that gun out so fast."

The doctor said, "Anybody to look after him?"

Mulvane had thought about that, wondering if he ought to put Joe Smith in the hotel. In Wickburg, though, Smith had no friends, and he would be better off out at the camp.

"I'm taking him out to the O'Leary ranch," Mulvane said.

"He shouldn't ride with that shoulder," the doctor warned. "Take him in a buckboard."

Crossing the street to the Ace High Livery, Mulvane rented a buckboard, tied the two mounts to the tailgate, and then walked the horses over to the physician's house. With the help of the physician he got Joe Smith into the buckboard, covered him with blankets, and then climbed up on the seat.

It was ten o'clock in the evening when they drove out of Wickburg, Mulvane letting the two horses in the traces set their own pace. Joe Smith said in a weak voice from the rear, "Damned better for us if we'd stayed at the camp, Mulvane. He's got you for the next target now."

Mulvane didn't say anything to this. He drove on in silence for some time, knowing tonight more than ever that he was going to be mighty lucky if he came out of this conflict alive. He knew that in all of his life he'd made no more implacable enemies than Von Dreber and the countess Hannau. Now with Trasker Flynn, the deadliest gunman in the West, definitely on Von Dreber's side, and with both Smiths unable to help, he would have to depend upon Charlie O'Leary and a few other nondescript gunslingers Charlie had been able to line up. The small ranchers like Meigs would not be of too much value if it came to open warfare.

They were halfway to the ranch when Joe Smith started to complain of thirst. Undoubtedly a mild fever had set in as an aftermath of the wound.

"We pass any water along here?" the gunman asked.

Mulvane remembered that there was a small creek running across the stage road a short distance ahead. Approaching the fording place, Mulvane accordingly swung the buckboard off the road and in under a clump of tall cottonwoods.

He stepped down from the buckboard and made

his way down to the creek, filled his hat full of water, and was returning to the buckboard when a half dozen riders pounded up the road, crossing the fording place, not seeing the buckboard concealed in the shadows of the cottonwoods.

Joe Smith said querulously when Mulvane came up with the water, "Who in hell was that?"

Holding the hat so that Joe Smith could drink Mulvane said, "Reckon we'll find out when they don't see us up ahead and turn back."

He had little doubt that the riders were some of Von Dreber's crew. Knowing that Mulvane was on the stage road with a wounded man, the Von Dreber riders had gone after them to finish them off.

Mulvane said after Joe Smith had finished drinking, "You figure you can use a gun?"

"Left hand's all right," the gunman told him.

Mulvane had tossed Joe Smith's gunbelt into the rear of the buckboard, and he pushed the belt toward the man now. Smith said quietly, "Von Dreber's bunch?"

"They'll be back," Mulvane assured him. "Keep down low."

Rapidly, he unhitched the team and led them down along the creek, along with his claybank and Smith's horse. He came back hurriedly to climb into the buckboard.

"How many?" Joe Smith asked.

"Six," Mulvane told him. "They figure there's one of us."

"Flynn with them?" Joe Smith asked.

Mulvane stared up the road over which the six Von Dreber men had just ridden, and then he shook his head. He didn't think this was the kind of work Flynn would do. Very possibly McAdams would be behind it, lining up the Von Dreber riders who were in town and sending them out after him.

It was fully fifteen minutes later when the six riders cantered back up the road in the direction of the creek. They came on slowly as they neared the creek.

"They figure they lost us somewhere along here," Joe Smith whispered as he crouched in the buckboard.

Mulvane held the gun steady in his hand, balancing it on the buckboard seat in front of him. He said nothing as he watched the riders split into two groups, one moving upstream and the other downstream in their direction.

"Not too bad now," Joe Smith chuckled.

The three men who were coming in their direction were moving past the grove of cottonwoods when one of them suddenly swerved in toward the trees to have a better look. He came to within thirty feet of the buckboard before spotting it, and then he let out a whoop, the gun booming in his hand.

Mulvane fired back at the flash of the gun and saw his man slump forward in the saddle. Then he rolled out of the buckboard and darted forward, dropping down behind the trees on the fringe of the grove.

The man who'd been hit was riding off, his body bouncing loosely in the saddle. The two other men swung in around the grove, trying to make a circuit of it, but then Joe Smith's pistol began to bark. Mulvane couldn't see whether either of them had been hit because they were now swinging out wide around the grove.

The three men who'd gone in the opposite direction had now swung back and were driving down along the creek, pounding across the stage road. As they spread out Mulvane lined his gun on the man in the middle and squeezed on the trigger. He saw the horse go by, riderless.

He sent two more shots, then, at the riders who were driving past the grove trying to get out of range of his pistol. The two who'd swung around behind Joe Smith tried to break in on the opposite side now, but Mulvane raced back to the buckboard and when both he and Smith opened with their pistols, knocking another man from the saddle, the lone rider kept going, headed back in the direction of Wickburg.

"That'll be it," Mulvane said as he pushed fresh charges into his gun. "Three of them hit. They won't want any more of this."

"Damned good thing I was thirsty," Joe Smith murmured. "If they had us out in the open it might not have been so easy."

When the remaining riders made no attempt to come back toward the grove, Mulvane moved forward on foot, searching along the creek where he'd knocked the last man from his horse. He found him sprawled in the gravel, hands reaching down toward the water. There was a bullet through his head. When Mulvane struck a match and held it close to his face he didn't recognize the man.

"A few more of 'em won't take Von Dreber's money anymore," Joe Smith said when Mulvane came back to the buckboard.

Hitching up the buckboard horses again, they started off, and it was nearly midnight when they rode up to the line shack, Charlie O'Leary coming out sleepily, and staring as Mulvane helped Joe Smith out of the buckboard.

"Clear a bunk inside," Mulvane ordered. "We have a wounded man here."

"Flynn?" Charlie O'Leary asked and Mulvane nodded.

"Winged me in the shoulder," Joe Smith mumbled.

After they'd gotten Joe Smith onto one of the bunks and comfortable Mulvane went outside with his blankets and tarpaulin. He was spreading them on the ground when Charlie said glumly,

"Both our top hands down now, Mulvane. What happens next? Our crowd here is gettin' kind o' worried."

"They should be trying a big push sooner or later," Mulvane observed. "Von Dreber's not a patient man and now he has Trasker Flynn with him."

"They make a big push on us," Charlie muttered, "an' we're finished. Von Dreber, Grimes an' the others know how strong we are now. They'll line up twice as many riders as before an' go right to hell over us."

Mulvane spread his blankets, got a smoke going, and then sat down. As he puffed on the cigarette he said, "Any place near here you could move the stock so Von Dreber couldn't grab it too quickly?"

Charlie thought for a moment. "Echo Canyon," he said. "Seven-eight miles from here. We could run 'em in there an' they'd be pretty safe fer a week anyway."

Mulvane nodded, "Get the stock rolling in the morning," he said. "Take the crew with you."

Charlie O'Leary stared at him. "What's the deal?" he asked finally.

Mulvane stretched himself out on the blanket, the cigarette in his mouth, and said softly, "Von Dreber and the big ranchers are too strong for us. Our only chance is to split them up."

Charlie laughed shortly. "Easy to say," he observed. "Damned site harder to do, Mulvane."

"We can try," Mulvane smiled. "If Grimes and the other ranchers learn that Von Dreber plans to take over every foot of rangeland around here, including their own, they'll drop him, won't they?"

"They'll drop him," Charlie nodded. "Have a hell of a time trying to prove it to Grimes, though."

Mulvane thought about that as he puffed on his cigarette, and then he said softly, "Reckon it can be done, Charlie. Get the stock out of here. Leave a man to watch Joe Smith. I'm going to have a talk with Grimes."

"You talked to him before," Charlie said. "It didn't do any damned good."

"This is another time." Mulvane smiled as he lay back and looked up at the stars.

CHAPTER 15

Before dawn the next morning Charlie O'Leary and the small ranchers had the stock moving in the direction of Echo Canyon. Mulvane had his breakfast with Joe Smith and a rancher who'd offered to remain behind until he was able to move with the others.

The blond gunman was stiff and wan but in fairly good spirits. "Hear you're movin' the stock out," he said to Mulvane as he sipped his coffee. "We're not running, are we?"

"Running today," Mulvane said. "There'll be time to fight tomorrow."

Finishing his breakfast, he saddled the claybank and rode directly to Grimes' Slash G. The squat, blunt-jawed Grimes was watching one of his riders break a horse in the corral as Mulvane rode up. The Slash G riders looked at Mulvane, hard-eyed, as he stepped down from the saddle.

Grimes said sourly, "Reckon you know you're not wanted around here, mister."

"Like a word with you," Mulvane smiled.

Grimes stared at him and then nodded briefly and walked back to the porch, Mulvane following him, leading the claybank. When they were out of hearing of the men Grimes said stiffly, "Say it, and then get out."

"Reckon I told you before," Mulvane began, "that Von Dreber intends to drive out O'Leary's crew and then work on you big ranchers one by one until he's taken over the whole range."

"Maybe you said it," Grimes nodded, "and I didn't believe a damn word of it."

"What if I can prove it?" Mulvane smiled. "Would you believe it then?"

Grimes looked at him and then he said, "Go ahead and talk, mister."

Mulvane spoke for several minutes and when he'd finished Grimes rolled a cigarette, his square face hard. For one moment Mulvane thought the rancher was going to turn down his proposition, and then the rancher said tersely, "I'll be there, and you'd better not try to pull any damned tricks, mister."

"You'll have your proof," Mulvane told him.

He stepped into the saddle, then, lifted a hand to Grimes, and rode off, very pleased so far with his plan.

Before noon he rode into Wickburg, stepped into the hotel, and got himself a room on the second floor. He procured paper and pen from the hotel clerk and sat down in a corner of the lobby to compose his letter very carefully. Then he put the note into an envelope and went back to the stable at the rear of the hotel where he located the stable boy pitching hay to the claybank.

For two dollars he persuaded the boy to ride

out to the Von Dreber castle and deliver the letter, personally, to the Countess Hannau. Coming out of the stable, then, he stepped into the hotel dining room, had his lunch, and went upstairs to his room.

An hour later, watching from the rear window of the hotel, he saw the stable boy return from his errand. It was two o'clock in the afternoon when he heard the light knock on his door. When he opened it Hilda Hannau stood there in riding clothes, puzzlement in her blue eyes. She wore a white blouse with fawn-colored riding pants, and her blonde hair was tucked in under the black, flat-crowned hat.

"Come in," Mulvane said. He closed the door after her when she'd stepped inside, and said, "You got my letter?"

The Countess Hannau stared at him. "You Americans change your minds very quickly, Herr Mulvane," she observed. "Are you serious about this?"

"Sit down," Mulvane told her, nodding toward a chair near the wall. He sat down on the edge of the bed and said, "Like to know what the whole deal is before I make up my mind. I don't figure on getting paid a hundred dollars and then riding out of here with nothing else."

"You mean—you'll stay?" Hilda Hannau asked him, "after we are successful?"

"Some things I want to know first," Mulvane

stated. "Way I look at it, Von Dreber will not stop after he takes over the ranges of these small men he's been fighting."

"No—no," the Countess Hannau said impatiently. "All of it."

Mulvane rubbed his jaw. "The big ranchers won't just walk out as easy as that," he observed. "Men like Grimes have been here a long time."

"They will have to go," the Countess informed him. "That has been the Colonel's plan from the beginning. First the little ones and then the big ones, one by one. They will have to go."

"They'll fight," Mulvane told her.

"We shall be hiring more men," Hilda Hannau said. "Men like yourself and Herr Flynn. They will make it possible."

Mulvane nodded, "And that's the way Von Dreber has it figured?" he said softly. "That's the way it was to be right from the start? He's taking over the whole damned business?"

"We'll need that much territory," the Countess told him. "You can be one of his lieutenants." She was speaking in a soft voice now, her blue eyes warm. "I am so glad you wrote me the note, Herr Mulvane, and that you have changed your mind. Was it because of Herr Flynn?"

Mulvane smiled at her. "Herr Flynn didn't scare me one damned bit," he said, and then he walked over to the wall and knocked on it with his knuckles.

The Countess Hannau stared at him curiously. "Why did you do that?" she asked.

Mulvane didn't have to reply, because a moment later Ed Grimes strode into the room, his face white with anger, heavy jaws clenched.

"Madam," the rancher said, his voice shaking, "if you were a man you'd be dead this minute. Now you can go back to your damned castle and tell Von Dreber that from now on he goes it alone against the rustlers, and that if he tries to take one foot of our range the bunch of us will band up and burn him out."

Hilda Hannau was staring at him incredulously, and then she looked at Mulvane, all the warmth gone from her eyes.

"It was a trick," she said in a low voice. "It was all a trick. My coming here was a trick."

Mulvane nodded soberly. "It was a trick," he admitted. He turned to Grimes and said, "You satisfied?"

"I'm satisfied," Grimes growled. Then he pointed a thick finger at the Countess Hannau and said, bitterly, "You tell Von Dreber he won't get a rider from me. If he tries to make trouble he'll find he's run into a hornet's nest."

The rancher strode out of the room, then, and Mulvane said easily, "Reckon that's it, Countess."

"I'll kill you," Hilda Hannau whispered. "I'll kill you, Herr Mulvane."

"Send Flynn if he wants to come," Mulvane told her. He put on his hat.

"I'll see you crawling in the dust," Hilda Hannau hissed.

"You might see me dead," Mulvane said, "but you won't see me crawling, ma'am."

He walked out of the hotel room, then, and down into the street, turning up toward the El Dorado. As he was going into the saloon he saw the Countess Hannau riding by at a furious pace, and he realized now that the die was cast. Flynn would come and probably Von Dreber and his crew would come, too, before this day was over. The whole business would be resolved before morning.

Rosslyn Elder was going over the receipts with one of her bartenders when Mulvane came in. She looked at him for a moment and nodded, and then crossed to meet him. He sat down at a table after ordering a beer from one of the bartenders.

Rosslyn said as she sat down across from him, "You're not out with O'Leary?"

"O'Leary's moving the stock up into a place called Echo Canyon," Mulvane explained. "They'll be safe enough for the time."

"How safe will they be," Rosslyn asked, "if Von Dreber and the ranchers bottle him up in the Canyon? I know the place. There's not enough grass there to graze a herd for more than a few days."

"They won't be bottled up," Mulvane assured her. "The big ranchers no longer back Von Dreber. He's alone in this and he's no longer big enough to go it alone."

Rosslyn was staring at him. "Grimes and the others pulled out?" she asked.

Mulvane nodded, and he told her how he'd gotten both Hilda Hannau and Grimes to come into town with Grimes concealed in the room next to the one he'd rented himself, and able to hear everything being said through the thin partitions.

Rosslyn was silent after he'd finished and then she said, "The small ranchers are safe. Von Dreber won't be strong enough to go after them now as long as they know enough to unite."

"The way I figured it," Mulvane nodded.

"What about you?" Rosslyn asked.

Mulvane sipped his beer. "What about me?" he countered.

"She said she'd have you killed, didn't she?"

He put the beer glass down. "She did," he nodded.

"That means Flynn will be here, and no doubt Von Dreber, himself. What are you going to do?"

Mulvane shrugged. "If Trasker Flynn wants me," he said, "he'll have his chance."

"You can't fight all of them," Rosslyn protested.

"Reckon Flynn will come first," Mulvane told

her. "It's his way. He never figured he needed help before."

"If he doesn't kill you the others will," Rosslyn said wearily. "Can't you see that?"

"I'm not dead, yet," Mulvane smiled, "and there's been a hell of a lot have tried."

"McAdams, too," Rosslyn tried to tell him. "He's been in with Von Dreber right from the start. You don't think he'll let you just ride out of here?"

"I'll ride when I'm ready," Mulvane said, and he saw the shadow come to her face.

"You always have to ride," she murmured. "Your kind always has to ride."

He had time on his hands this afternoon after he'd left her, and he went back to the hotel to the room he'd rented for the day. Very coolly, he locked the door, slid a chair under the doorknob, unbuckled his gunbelt, and slept soundly for four hours.

He awoke at dusk because someone was knocking on the door, knocking vigorously. Drawing his gun from the holster on the bedpost he stepped to one side of the door and said, "All right."

"Open up," Charlie O'Leary said.

Frowning, Mulvane pushed aside the chair and unlocked the door. As Charlie O'Leary came into the darkened room Mulvane crossed to the window, drew the blinds carefully, and then touched a match to the lamp, making sure that his silhouette was not revealed against the blind.

"What brings you here, Charlie?" he asked.

"Miss Elder sent a rider out to Echo Canyon," Charlie growled. "What in hell do you mean by tryin' to buck this whole crowd by yourself?"

"Might just be Trasker Flynn," Mulvane smiled. "It might not get any further than that."

Charlie grimaced. "Hear you were able to split up Von Dreber and the big ranchers," he said. "Is it for good?"

"For good," Mulvane told him, remembering how Ed Grimes had left this room hours earlier. "Reckon you boys can run the stock back to your own ranches now. They'll be safe enough. If Von Dreber tries to hit at you you'll know you have to get together again."

Charlie nodded. "We're obliged to you for this, Mulvane," he said quietly, "but now what?"

"What?" Mulvane smiled.

"Why not be smart," Charlie said, "an' ride to hell out of here. You know how bad Flynn is with a gun, an' Von Dreber will never rest till he has you shot to pieces. If not by Flynn, by somebody else."

Mulvane said easily, "Reckon I'll wait around, Charlie."

"You were always the stubborn one," Charlie O'Leary growled.

"You were pretty stubborn, too, about not riding out of here," Mulvane reminded him, "when Von Dreber burned you out. We're both stubborn ones, Charlie."

Charlie nodded. "All right," he said. "If they want to make a fight out o' this they'll have one, an' it won't be just your gun."

Mulvane said, "No call for you to stay, Charlie. It'll be between Flynn and myself."

"An' there'll be some other damned coyotes around," Charlie said grimly, "like McAdams. It won't hurt you to have another gun nearby."

Mulvane put a hand on the small rancher's shoulder and he said, "Supper first, Charlie."

They left the hotel, had their supper in the hotel dining room, and then went out on the street.

"You figure Flynn's in town yet?" Charlie asked.

"He'll be coming in," Mulvane assured him, and then they saw Von Dreber's buckboard coming down the street with Von Dreber and the Countess Hannau on the seat. They stood in a darkened alley way watching the buckboard go by, seeing it pull up in front of the hotel.

Charlie said, "She's come in for the kill, Mulvane. This one she wants to see."

Mulvane nodded and said nothing. They walked on up to the El Dorado, Charlie O'Leary looking into each saloon as they passed by, trying to spot Trasker Flynn. As they walked Mulvane smelled the rain in the night air. The day had been exceptionally hot, and it was apparent that a change was due.

Flynn was not in the El Dorado, either. As they stood up at the bar waiting for the bartender to serve them, Rosslyn Elder came down the stairs, crossed to where they stood, and said to Mulvane, "You're still alive."

"Still alive," Mulvane smiled. "Flynn been in?"

"Not yet," she said. "I've seen some of Von Dreber's crew drifting in and out. You know what that means?"

"What about McAdams?" Mulvane asked.

"He hasn't been in, either," Rosslyn told him.

"You didn't have to send for Charlie," Mulvane observed.

"Swallow some of your pride," Rosslyn said quietly. "You'll need him and you'll need more than him."

"We'll see," Mulvane told her. He had a drink with Charlie and then they sat at one of the card tables, Mulvane playing solitaire while Charlie watched and waited nervously.

After an hour had passed Charlie O'Leary said grimly, "You're damned sure Flynn's comin' after you alone? Could be they're plannin' to set you up now, one way or the other. Reckon that's the way I look at it."

Mulvane shook his head. "Flynn won't be afraid of me," he said.

"Von Dreber wants you dead," Charlie scowled, "an' he don't give a damn about Flynn. It's you he wants. I figure they'll try to set you up before this night's over."

The little old man who had befriended Mulvane on the night of his fight with Von Dreber bustled into the room now and came up to their table. He said in a low voice, "Mr. Flynn went into the hotel to meet with Von Dreber."

Mulvane put a silver dollar down on the table and he said, "You're my man tonight. Watch them."

The old man grinned, snatched up the coin, and left the saloon. From his table Mulvane saw Rosslyn Elder watching him from the bar and he saw the worry in her face.

Neil McAdams came into the saloon, paused for a few minutes to talk with a man near the bar, ascertained Mulvane's location, and then went out. Charlie said, "They're plannin' the whole damned thing, Mulvane. Flynn's in town, but he ain't comin' alone."

"We'll see," Mulvane said.

A cool breeze was pushing down from the mountains, driving away the heat of the day. Now as he sat at the card table with Charlie O'Leary he heard the first faint pattering of rain outside.

Charlie got up from the table and walked to the door to look outside. The wind was beginning to whip down the street, rattling loose signs.

Mulvane continued to play solitaire, his face expressionless as he laid out the cards.

The floorman came over to watch for a few moments and he said, "A wet night, Mr. Mulvane."

Mulvane nodded. The floorman watched for a while and then moved on. Rosslyn Elder came over and sat down across from him. She said, an edge to her voice, "I can have someone bring your horse to the back door and you can ride out with no one knowing the difference. This range war is over. What can you accomplish by staying here?"

Mulvane looked at her across the table. "Reckon I'll stay," he said.

"In six months," Rosslyn said, "Von Dreber's whole plan will be finished. He'll fall of his own weight. You can come back here."

"To you?" Mulvane asked gently.

He saw her lips tighten. "All right, to me," she said.

"It won't work," Mulvane told her. "I have to move. When a thing is over I have to move away from it."

He saw the tiredness come to her face and she nodded, understanding how it was.

He said, "There are good men in this town."

Rosslyn shook her head. "Don't feel sorry for me," she said, and then she got up and walked back to the bar, her figure tall and straight, shoulders erect. Mulvane had his respect for her.

There was a crash of thunder outside and then a sign blew down somewhere along the street, making a loud bang as it struck the walk. Charlie came back inside and said, "Somebody standing outside the hotel. Can't make out who it is."

"They'll get wet they go out in the rain," Mulvane said, and Charlie snorted in disgust.

"Man should be a little more damned serious about a thing like this," he growled.

"How should a man die?" Mulvane asked, "smiling or crying?"

Charlie just grumbled again and walked toward the bar for a bottle and a glass. Mulvane could see that the waiting was getting on the little man's nerves. Charlie O'Leary wasn't afraid of a fight and he wasn't afraid to die, but he didn't like waiting, and Mulvane wondered if this was Trasker Flynn's way: to keep him waiting here, to keep him in suspense, to break his nerve.

Calmly, Mulvane shuffled the cards and laid them out on the table, solitaire fashion. His hands were steady and there was no emotion in his face.

It was nine thirty in the evening with the rain coming down steady now, the wind having abated somewhat. He could hear the rain splashing in the muddied street outside. A horse went by, hoofs sloshing.

Possibly because of the inclement weather, the El Dorado was only half-filled with half the card tables on the main floor unoccupied. The top floor gambling room was not even open. Two of the four bartenders behind the long bar were having an avid conversation, finding nothing else to do.

At ten o'clock the little old man to whom Mulvane had given the dollar bustled into the gambling house, his faded gray coat splattered with rain, and excitement in his face. He could scarcely get the words out he was so excited, and as he was stumbling Mulvane said to him, "Easy, Grandpa."

The old man got it straight then. He had a message from Trasker Flynn who was now on the hotel porch. The old man repeated each word slowly and clearly so that Mulvane could not possibly misconstrue it.

"Mr. Flynn would be obliged if you would meet him out in front of the Wyoming Saloon in ten minutes."

The old man showed him the silver dollar Flynn had given to him to deliver the message.

"Ten minutes," he repeated, faded old eyes glistening.

Mulvane nodded.

"What—what'll I tell him?" the old man asked.

"Tell him I'll be there," Mulvane said, and he went on playing cards as the old man bolted out of the saloon, leaving the doors swinging.

Charlie O'Leary came back from the bar

carrying a bottle and two glasses. "What did he want?" Charlie asked suspiciously.

"Flynn sent a message that he'd like to meet me in front of the Wyoming in ten minutes," Mulvane said.

Charlie O'Leary sat down, still keeping one hand on the bottle. "All right," he said. "All right."

Mulvane went on playing cards.

"What in hell did you tell him?" Charlie snapped.

Mulvane smiled. "I told him I'd be there," he said, and now he had the card he wanted in this solitaire game, the eight of spades, and the whole game worked out neatly and in order. He placed one card on top of the other until he had four small piles in front of him, aces on the bottoms, kings on tops, all the colors in order.

He pushed back the chair then, smiling faintly, thinking how different life was. In real life nothing ever seemed to be in order; nothing worked out the way a man hoped it would work out. You took life as it came, and if it came the wrong way you took it anyway, and you didn't complain. You never complained. It was the way of a man.

CHAPTER 16

Charlie O'Leary was saying, "I'll be behind you, Mulvane. Flynn ain't comin' alone. The others will be close by."

Mulvane said, "Don't take any flying lead, Charlie."

Then he walked up to the bar where Rosslyn Elder was watching. He said, "I'm moving out. Flynn's waiting for me up the street."

She had nothing to say to him now, but she said it with her eyes. She had her hand on the bar and Mulvane placed his on top of hers for a moment, and then he walked away. He went out on the porch and he stood there for some time watching the rain, letting his eyes grow accustomed to the dim light. He wondered how Von Dreber had persuaded Trasker Flynn to do it in this manner. He was positive Flynn would have much preferred walking into the El Dorado and calling him out. He was convinced that Von Dreber, McAdams and especially the woman, had persuaded Flynn to do it this way. If Flynn knocked him down now the fight would be over right then and there. On the other hand if he bested Flynn, Von Dreber and the others would go for him, and this he had to watch if he expected to live through this night.

Charlie O'Leary said at his elbow, "There's an alley right near the Wyoming. Watch that. I'll be comin' up on the other side o' the street."

Mulvane remembered the alley, the same one up which he'd chased Jug Streiber, eventually catching up with him in the back room of the Wyoming.

When he looked along the boardwalk he could see the porch of the hotel nearly a hundred yards away. A man was coming down the steps, moving in under the protective wood awning so that he would not get wet.

"Luck," Charlie said.

Mulvane nodded and turned up the street. He walked without haste, noticing how the rain was still sweeping down the street in sheets, streaming off the awning overhead, forming almost a veil so that he could hardly see across the road.

He had to step out into the rain only once when he came to a small intersection. When he ducked under the awning on the opposite side of the street he saw a man walking toward him from the direction of the hotel.

The town of Wickburg seemed to be deserted this night, and he saw no living thing as he walked down the street except a big, yellow tomcat perched on a window sill.

Patches of light from the houses on the street lay along the walk, and he could see Trasker Flynn going through one patch and then another.

Now he noticed that Flynn had stopped a short distance beyond the Wyoming Saloon, not more than a dozen feet from the alley.

Flynn stood with one shoulder against an awning upright with a cascade of water falling from the awning overhead. Mulvane walked on until he was thirty feet from Flynn, and then he, too, stopped. He said softly, "That you, Trasker?"

"All right," Flynn said. "Close enough."

"You picked a wet night, Trasker," Mulvane said, humor in his voice.

"It's wet," Flynn agreed.

"You wanted to see me," Mulvane said. He stood in the center of the walk, his hands at his sides, feet braced on the wood. He noticed now that Flynn had pushed away from the post and was standing a foot or so from it, his coat open, the big Navy Colt clear.

Mulvane waited, and then Trasker Flynn said, "You insulted a lady-friend of mine, Mr. Mulvane."

Mulvane smiled. "If it wasn't that," he said, "it would be something else, Trasker."

"Do you wish to apologize?" Flynn asked him.

"Draw your gun," Mulvane said.

The cat which Mulvane had seen on the window sill had followed him down the walk, and coming up behind him the cat now rubbed itself against his boot. Surprised, Mulvane, not having seen the cat, stepped to one side quickly, just as Trasker

Flynn's gun spoke, the orange-red flame winking toward him.

His own gun boomed a trifle of a second later as Flynn's bullet missed him completely. Mulvane fired once and then again. The first bullet knocked Flynn back against the awning upright. The second one spun him around so that he clung to the post as he fell out into the mud of the road, his gun still in his hand. The gun roared again as he fell, the lead plowing into the soft mud.

Gun in hand, Mulvane reached down and stroked the head of the cat which had saved his life this night, and at that moment he saw a man suddenly step out of the alley, a gun in his hand. Even in the shadows there he recognized the chunky figure of Neil McAdams.

McAdams was unable to get a single shot off. A gun started to bark across the street, once, twice, three times. McAdams fell to his knees, clutching his stomach with his left hand, the gun sagging in his right. As he fell forward on hands and knees his shoulders heaved and the hat fell from his head.

As McAdams went down on the walk three men broke out of the alley behind him and came charging down toward Mulvane. The man in the middle was big, heavy-shouldered, and Mulvane recognized him immediately as Von Dreber.

The man to Von Dreber's right fired first, his

lead grazing Mulvane's left cheek. Mulvane dropped this man with the first shot and then swiveled the gun over to Von Dreber, firing twice as Von Dreber's gun boomed.

The big Prussian seemed to lose his balance. He stumbled forward, the gun banging again and the lead going into the wood in front of him, and then he pitched on his face with a sickening thud as Charlie O'Leary opened up with his gun from across the road.

The third man wasn't hit, but with both Von Dreber and his companion down he turned and darted back into the alley. Von Dreber was down but he wasn't dead even though Mulvane was convinced that both shots from his pistol had caught Von Dreber in vital places.

The big rancher tried to crawl toward him on the damp wood. He crawled three feet and then he tried to lift his head; his shoulders heaved once, and then he was still.

Charlie O'Leary came in out of the rain, gun in hand, had a look at McAdams, and then he rolled Von Dreber over on his back, and said to Mulvane, "Damned war's over."

Mulvane walked on ahead to pull Flynn's body back onto the walk and out of the rain. Flynn had been struck twice in the chest and either bullet would have killed him. He stood there for a moment looking down at the man, sadness in his face.

Looking up the street toward the hotel he saw the Countess Hannau standing on the porch, staring in his direction. She'd seen the entire fight; she'd seen both Flynn and Von Dreber downed, and now she saw Mulvane standing on the walk, blood trickling from his cut cheek.

For several long moments they looked at each other across the distance, Mulvane standing in a patch of light, and Hilda Hannau revealed clearly in the light from the hotel window. She stood very stiff, and then quite suddenly Mulvane saw her shoulders sag, and she turned and walked back into the hotel.

The doorways were filled with faces as Mulvane and Charlie O'Leary walked back toward the El Dorado. Rosslyn Elder had come outside and was standing on the walk, looking in their direction, relief coming into her face as Mulvane came into sight.

Mulvane said to Charlie O'Leary, "I'm obliged, Charlie."

"My fight more than yours," Charlie told him.

"You all right?" Rosslyn asked when she saw the blood on Mulvane's face.

"Just a scratch," he said, and then he walked with her to the bar.

"A drink," she said, "wouldn't hurt you now."

Mulvane agreed. He stood there holding a bandanna against the cut cheek, and he had his drink. The fiery liquor was warm in his chest and stomach. At his elbow Charlie O'Leary said, "All over now, Mulvane."

Mulvane nodded, Rosslyn Elder watching him.

"You'll ride on tomorrow?" she asked.

"I'll ride on," Mulvane told her.

She expected it, and she said nothing, accepting it the way it was, resignation in her face now.

"It's best," Mulvane said.

"I know," she said.

He knew it, also. It was the only way for him. He had to go on, to move, to ride over one hill so that he could see another. For him it was the only way, a way he'd made for himself, and a way in which he had to walk all the days of his life.

Center Point Large Print
600 Brooks Road / PO Box 1
Thorndike, ME 04986-0001 USA

(207) 568-3717

US & Canada:
1 800 929-9108
www.centerpointlargeprint.com